Dead Frog on the Porch

"Shady scientists, fraudulent frogs, and two terrific twins add up to a delightful mystery. Cynthia and Jane are fearless in their quest to end 'crimes against amphibians.'

"This story is full of outsized characters, outrageous creatures and a sweet goofy humor that propels each page. Tons of fun!"

—*Teresa Toten*
Governor General Awards nominee 2001
Governor General Awards finalist 2006

"Readers who enjoy a good laugh and a good mystery will devour this uproarious, fast-paced story in which the feisty twin sisters Cyd and Jane take a megabyte out of crime! It is Nancy Drew for the iPod generation!

"Markley's début novel, filled with suspense and zany humour and told with pizzazz, ushers in a new voice in the mystery genre. A sure winner!"

—*Shenaaz Nanji*
Governor General Award Finalist 2008.

Dead Frog
on the Porch

A Megabyte Mystery
by Jan Markley

gumboot books

www.gumbootbooks.com

Library and Archives Canada Cataloguing in Publication

Markley, Jan, 1961-
Dead frog on the porch : a megabyte mystery / by Jan Markley.

ISBN 978-1-926691-06-0

I. Title.

PS8626.A7537D42 2009   jC813'.6

C2009-905821-9

Cover Illustration by Mike Linton
Book Design by Crystal Stranaghan

With special thanks to Jared Hunt and Melanie Jackson for all their editorial guidance and advice.

www.gumbootbooks.com
Printed and bound in the USA on acid-free paper that contains no material from old-growth forests, using ink that is safe for children.

To my late father, Lyall Markley, and my mother, Nadia Markley, who encouraged my love of reading and writing from a young age. JM

Chapter One
The First Frog

If I'd known that killing my twin sister's frog would lead to such a chain of events, I would've been more careful. Not that I killed it on purpose. It was an accident, more like frog-slaughter. It certainly wasn't premeditated frogicide.

The mystery we unravelled made my sister and me heroes; well, heroines to be exact. It was the first summer our mom and dad didn't send us to day camps, now that we were twelve. Plus, we were writing a mystery novel.

Little did we know that we would become part of an adventure.

It started on the hottest day of summer – a two-Popsicle kinda day. We'd been picking cabbage from the garden, eating a bit and feeding it to Jane's rabbit. I wanted to jump on the giant inflated tire tube on the lawn in the middle of the yard, so I vaulted down the back porch steps.

Halfway down, I felt a crunch under my foot. I thought it was a piece of cabbage and I kept going.

I jumped on the tire tube and waited for Jane to join me. After a few jumps, I noticed she was sitting on the bottom porch step, stooped over.

Then Jane screeched.

"What's the matter?" I yelled back.

"Frogzilla!"

I sprinted back. Jane covered her face with

her hands as she hunched over her pet frog. Jane's shoulders trembled. I crouched. My heart sank to my stomach when I saw Frogzilla. He was as flat as the spatula we used when we tried to fry an egg on the sidewalk the other day. We'd told our mom it was a science experiment but she wasn't impressed.

"I'm sorry," I groaned, and checked my heel for remnants of my sister's most recent pet. When I stepped on Jane's frog, it felt wet and firm like cabbage crunched between my bare toes. The bottom of my foot was clean, but my stomach churned. "I think we can save him," Jane squeaked. She tried not to cry.

The frog was dead, doorknob dead. It was hopeless. Little frog legs were separated from a now-flat frog body. Purple stringy frog guts were all over the bottom porch step. Good thing I wasn't a cow or all four of my guts would have been grossed out.

Everyone thinks cows have four stomachs but

really, it's one stomach with four chambers. I learned that in science camp last year – what a snore.

"If I can just get his arms and legs to go back inside his body," Jane said, as if in a trance. She fought to hold back a sob but lost the fight. My twin sister shuddered, then fell silent.

I stood there, not knowing what to say or do. I did know, however, that Jane should stop touching the frog. Wasn't there a rule Mom told us about touching dead animals?

Unless of course the animal was in Mom's lab and soaking in formaldehyde. "I don't think you should touch him. Why don't we just throw him out?"

Jane looked at me through her tears. If looks could kill, I'd be in the same condition as Frogzilla.

"Cyd, he deserves a proper burial," she said, brushing away the tears with the back of her hand. Oh, the germs on that hand!

"A burial befitting a frog? That would be one flat box," I said before I could stop myself. Jane glared at me. I realized it was one of those times my mother had told me about, when I should have thought before I spoke. *Not everyone appreciates your razor sharp wit,* I could hear her say. *But it's a big part of my charm,* I would reply... well, sometimes.

"I didn't do it on purpose. It was an accident."

Jane didn't seem to hear me, and rearranged the frog bits as if she planned surgery.

"We can always get another one from the lake."

"Don't even think of blogging about this." She aimed the frog-touching-finger at me.

"No, I wouldn't. I couldn't." I jumped out of finger-poking range. But I already had the blog entry title: *Cabbage Woes not Cabbage Rolls.* Better yet: *Don't be a Heel, Local Frog will be missed.* However, I didn't

10

even have my digital camera, so it wouldn't be worth a blog entry without a photo to upload. The title of the next blog entry was meant to be: *Bin There Done That: garbage cans on a roll after big wind blows in.* The dead frog headline would be way better.

Jane sighed, put her face in her hands, and cried more.

I put my arm around her shoulder. Since the whole thing was my fault, I felt doubly bad. We sat there for a long time not saying anything. I could feel the heat from the sun on the back of my ears, but didn't dare suggest we re-apply sunscreen.

A mosquito landed on my arm. I didn't move. It jabbed my skin. I felt the sting as it sucked my blood. I wanted to swat it, but Jane had just started to calm down. I brushed my arm against my leg to get the mosquito off, and it burst.

Blood stained my arm. Jane looked at it, looked

11

back at Frogzilla, and shivered.

Jane was crazy about animals. That's why she refused to dissect her frog in science class, even though it was already dead. She convinced the teacher that she could do it virtually through a computer program she found on the Internet. A site called kids-against-dissecting-frogs.com or something like that. Jane got a "B" which pulled down her average, but according to her, it was the kind of "B" that you could feel good about.

Still sobbing, Jane scooped up all the parts of her frog and went to bury it in the woody area in the backyard. I got a garden spade and joined her there. From experience, I knew that she usually felt better after a burial.

Jane's crying let up as she concentrated on digging the hole with the spade. Part of the backyard was like a miniature forest. Sunk into the ground, it was filled with trees, bushes, and flowers. This is where we would sometimes write our mystery novel plots. We were writing a Nancy Drew book, except we weren't going to call it that, of course. We were going to call it Stories From the Cyd Files. Or the Jane Files. We always argued over that.

I pretended to be Nancy Drew. My sister alternated between Nancy's two friends George and Bess, depending on the plot twist. I think Jane was more like Bess, timid. I was good with words and Jane was good with the computer. Not only did she know where the best home pages were, she found out there were conferences and professors who presented papers about Nancy Drew books. This was the only thing that kept our parents from sending us to science camp again. We told them we really wanted to analyze the plots and the characters. We didn't let on that we were always on the lookout for a mystery to solve.

13

When the hole was deep enough, Jane put her frog in it. I pushed the earth into the hole and saw Frogzilla for the last time. The earth was cool and I felt a worm wiggle. Jane found two twigs and, with a couple of pieces of grass, tied them together to make a cross.

She was crying the whole time. Boy, did I feel bad.

One twin wasn't supposed to kill the other twin's frog. It's a law, or it should be. Mom always told us how lucky we were to have each other. I didn't feel very lucky, right then. I guess Jane didn't either, from the pained look on her face.

Jane put the twig cross on top of the mound and said a prayer. How did she know what a proper prayer would be for a frog? My parents weren't religious, but that didn't stop them from buying books for us on the religions of the world and taking us to their friends'

14

churches. I guess Jane just made up a prayer. Her face relaxed a bit, but she was still upset. I suggested we go inside as I tried to think of something to take her mind off her frog.

Mom was cooking dinner in a big pot. For some reason the sight of the stew bubbling made Jane all teary-eyed again. Jane didn't talk about her frog much after that. She promised me she wasn't mad, but the funny thing was, the next time we were on the Internet, she said she couldn't get to the Nancy Drew homepage. She said the site was down or something, a *likely* story. I didn't want the title of our next blog entry to be: *Unfortunate Sasquatch accident: Big Foot Crushes Twin.*

I vowed to make it up to her as I scratched that mosquito bite.

Chapter Two
My Favorite Amphibian

"Cynthia," Mom popped her head in the bathroom, "be extra nice to your sister today." Mom had heard all about the dead frog on the porch. Well, she'd heard about it from me because Jane didn't want to talk about it.

"I'm always nice," I whispered under my breath.

"Oh, and Cynthia," Mom called. "Please brush your hair before you go out."

I stared into the mirror and my reflection smirked back at me. Even on a good day, my hair looked like it had lost an argument with a brush.

"Okay, Mom."

I wasn't about to remind Mom that my name wasn't Cynthia anymore; my name was now Cyd. It was short for Cynthia and way cooler. Although Jane and I were identical twins, my hair looked like the old toothbrush Mom used to clean the silver. Jane's hair always looked neatly brushed. I took a stab at my hair with the brush.

We have red hair. It isn't bright red, more like henna or auburn. That makes us stand out even more than just being twins. I steam inside when I hear the words carrot top or fireball.

Jane just laughs. For some reason she thinks it's funny to be compared to a vegetable that grows underground or an inferno that could wipe out a small field of grain.

"And stay on the bike paths between here and the mall. I'm off to the lab," chirped Mom.

Mom and Dad were cancer research scientists and worked in the lab at the university. Dad was on sabbatical in England for the summer, so it was just the three of us. For the last two weeks of summer we would join Dad in England and travel around, but until then Mom worked and we were on our own. School had just got out and we were anxious to find some adventures to write about. But I knew the drill. We had to take care of the business with the dead frog.

"Hurry up, Cyd. I want to be there as soon as the pet store opens. I did a search on line of pet stores and there's a shortage of frogs this summer. We'll have to see what else they have," Jane said.

I'd offered to spring for the new pet to make up for the untimely death of her frog, as long as it wasn't

18

more than one week's allowance.

"Maybe we can stop by the lab on the way back and bike home with mom." I had a plan. At the lab, there would be an extra frog hopping around that the scientists didn't need. Jane would instantly fall in love with the frog, forget about Frogzilla and forgive me. That was the plan, but plans don't always turn out the way you want them to.

"Sure, sounds good. Let's go."

I slid my right foot into my shoe and something gross squelched through my toes. It was the familiar cold slimy feel of cat vomit. "No, not again!" I cried and grabbed at my shoe. "Hang on." It wasn't the first time that Yin had thrown up in my lucky red shoes, and I had a feeling, as I cleaned them out, that it wouldn't be the last. Even though she was Jane's cat, Yin always found my shoes when she needed to throw up. It's a good thing she's cute because what she lacks in digestive abilities she makes up for with beauty. I don't blame Yin. She has a chronic hairball problem.

We called her Yin because half of her face was white, with a black circle around her eye, and half was black. Her body was a combination of black and white patches. We came up with the name when we were five, but later found out that the concepts of *Yin* and *Yang* are opposites within a whole – kinda like Jane and me.

I much prefer books to animals. Books never throw up on you. I ran to the bathroom, cleaned my shoes with a wet towel, and put them on still damp. The way things had been going lately, there was no way I was going to leave without my lucky shoes.

We lived close to the university in a mid-sized city. Our route, as always, was to bike through the university campus. Last time, Jane showed me the building where they did medical experiments on animals. I hoped she wouldn't mention it today. I was afraid it would remind her of her frog.

"Hey, look. Stop!"

Jane pointed toward the back of a building. I stopped beside her. A man and a woman wearing winter gloves were carrying cages of cats and mice out of the building. They put them into the back of a truck marked *Empire Meats.*

"Why would an Empire Meats truck be here?" Jane asked.

"Maybe there's a reception."

"But they're taking animals out, not cheese platters in! Scientists don't wear those types of gloves. Let's get a little closer. Maybe we can see them better and hear what they are saying."

"Come on. Let's go." I grabbed her arm. This was just the kind of thing that would get her thinking about Frogzilla again. "It's probably nothing. Maybe they're taking them to another lab." I said that to distract Jane, but my mystery-writer senses tingled.

"Not in *that* truck. Shh, they'll hear us."

Jane had other ideas. She walked her bike around the side and flipped the kickstand down. Then she ducked down behind a clump of bushes. I ditched my bike and followed. I crouched beside her.

The air was still and we could hear everything they said. The sun shone like a magnifying glass on my head. I felt like an ant. I wished I hadn't left my sun hat at home.

"Okay, let's go. I think we have enough," said the man.

"We've got enough cats and mice, but we need frogs," said the woman. She put her hands on her hips and looked in the truck. "Frogs! How could we forget the frogs? The experiment will be on frogs. Let's get a couple of cages of frogs."

22

Could she say the word frog a few hundred more times? Frogs were Jane's favourite amphibians. I shot a glance at Jane, afraid she would be upset.

She was all right. Her eyes were glued to the scene like it was a giant flat-screen television. She listened to the conversation like her life depended on it, or should I say the life of a frog.

"It's too soon to start on the frogs. We have to test the formula on mammals first to see if it would have any adverse effects on people," said the man.

Adverse effects! What did that mean? I guessed they meant that bad things would happen. I tried to get closer.

"Then we'll try it on frogs," he said. "Besides, this is taking too long." He looked over his shoulder. "Someone may notice the truck. I thought I saw some kids on bikes."

"Kids on bikes. There are always kids on bikes.

It's a bike path, you nincompoop. Don't be a Nervous Nellie. Kids on bikes are the least of our worries if this experiment doesn't work out. This experiment will mean the difference between riches or jail time."

The man looked crushed. The woman softened. "Look, we don't want to have to come back a second time. It's the frogs that matter, isn't it?" she asked.

"All right. One cage full. Let's hurry. We've got to get going," he said. They went back into the building and propped the back door open with a cage full of mice.

"They're stealing cats, mice, and now frogs!" Jane exclaimed. "Who the heck are they? They're up to something. Quick, let's follow them. This is Mom's building."

I grabbed Jane's T-shirt as she bolted past me. "Are you nuts? These people could be dangerous. We don't know where they're going or what they're doing.

Besides, we're supposed to be going to the mall."

"Forget about the mall. That's kid's stuff. Nancy Drew would follow them," Jane whispered back to me as she ran for the door.

Well, I couldn't argue with that logic. Jane's voice was full of anguish, mixed with anger. It was a lethal combination if they knew my twin. Jane was halfway up the stairs before I caught up with her. When did she get so adventurous? Maybe she thought they would drop a frog and she could rescue it.

We followed them to the second floor. Jane crouched down by the entrance to the lab. The door was open a crack. She motioned me toward her. I leaned over behind her.

The culprits rushed between the cages. "This is crazy," I muttered, as I stood up and leaned my back against the cool brick wall. The sound of cages clanging echoed off the walls.

Jane jumped up. "Shh. Don't you recognise this lab? It's where they keep the animals. Mom showed it to us once – remember? Listen, I can hear them."

"Okay, Jane, that's it. Let's go. This is nuts. We shouldn't even be in here."

Jane held up her hand. "Stop being the big sister just because you were born two minutes before me. We have to find out what's going on so we can call the police." She put her ear closer to the door.

Put solidly in my place, I slouched against the wall. At first, we couldn't hear any animal sounds. Sweat dripped from my hair and it wasn't from the bike ride in the sun. Then the howling started.

Chapter Three
The Plot

The sounds of meowing and barking bounced off the walls. High-pitched cat cries like when I accidentally stepped on Yin's tail. Short, frantic yelps like you hear from the neighborhood dogs before a big thunderstorm. The frog croaking was the loudest sound. Cages rattled. We could hear voices again.

"What are they saying?" I asked Jane who was closer.

"They're talking about the lab. Do you think

27

they work with Mom?"

"How am I supposed to know that?" I hissed. "We follow two people who are stealing animals from a university lab and, all of a sudden, I'm supposed to know everything about them. You get mad at me for treating you like the younger twin, but you seem to think that being two minutes older gives me some special wisdom."

"Pipe down. You wanted to find a mystery – well, we've found one."

"I don't know if they work with Mom. Keep listening, maybe we'll find out."

"I can hear them again. Write this down," said Jane.

"Write it down? I didn't bring my amateur detective super spy sleuthing notebook!" I made that up, but it would be a cool thing to have.

Jane repeated what she heard. "Something

about ...'Now that we have the animals... uh ...Petri dish ... I can't hear very well'.

They're talking about frogs. 'We should have done this years ago... budget cutbacks... take the animals to the warehouse and hide them and do the experiments...'"

Jane jumped up. "Do you know what this means? Wait a minute." Jane tapped her fingers on her chin. "I saw this movie once where the bad guys released some kind of virus in the town's water supply and everyone got sick. Maybe they'll do it through the animals. That's it!" she hissed.

I grabbed Jane's arm and pulled her toward the stairs. "Or maybe they are frog lovers trying to save all the frogs from ending up in school science labs! This is no time for a movie review. For someone who wouldn't even dissect a frog, you're quite a scientist all of a sudden."

29

Jane's shoulders slumped and she pulled away from me. She put her ear back to the door. I could tell I'd hurt her feelings, but Jane's idea of a complicated mystery plot was, Nancy and Bess go camping and forget the can opener. I promised myself I would be more sensitive, what with the death of her frog and all.

"I can hear them again," she whispered. "They're saying '... have to be careful, lab partner can't suspect a thing, or we'll have to get lab partner out of the picture...' Who do you think they could mean?"

My stomach muscles tightened. Who was their lab partner? Could they mean Mom? How could Mom be involved in this? Before I could answer my own questions, we heard their footsteps clomp toward the door. I stood up. The doorknob turned. I grabbed Jane's arm. We ran to the end of the hall and hid behind a recycling bin.

The two thieves had trouble getting the cages through the doorway of the lab, and kept bashing them against the sides and swearing. Where's the swear jar when you need it? The croaking of the frogs drowned out their voices. I held my breath. What would they do if they saw us? The three new mosquito bites on my shin itched, but I didn't dare scratch them now.

The culprits struggled to the stairs; each carried two large cages of frogs. The sound of their footsteps as they stomped down the stairs faded into an eerie silence. Then they were gone.

We didn't move. We stayed crouched until we heard the door at the bottom of the stairs slam shut. I wanted to get out of there. My knees were trembling. I told myself it was because we'd squatted for so long.

"Let's dash." I yanked Jane up and headed for the stairwell. We slid down the stairs and nudged the door open. Sunshine struck my eyes like a dentist's light. But

I knew that any detective worth her weight in X-ray glasses would memorize the license plate number of the truck that pulled out. I shielded my eyes from the sun and read, I 8 MEAT. That wouldn't be too hard to remember!

The scientists, or thieves, or whoever they were, squealed out of the parking lot. They were gone. Our bikes were still there. We still had hours to go before we could meet Mom. We ditched the mall and headed home. As I pedaled, my heart beat in time with the man's words ... *have to get lab partner out of the picture...* What would Nancy do? Had we just overheard a murder plot? But whose murder?

Chapter Four
The Dough Man

"Nancy Drew would tell her dad." Jane pedalled hard to keep up with me.

It was the next day and Jane had talked about the animals all night. "Only if she's in danger," I yelled back into the wind. "We're not in danger and neither is Mom!" Or was she? I rode into the driveway and on into the backyard. I dropped my bike and faced Jane. I didn't want my sister to get carried away with this.

"Look, Nancy might tell George and Bess and

maybe even her goofy boyfriend, Ned Nickerson, but not her dad. He's a lawyer, remember? Too busy. That's why she has all that time to solve mysteries.

"We're not going to tell Mom until we have more information. She'll think we're making things up. You know what she says about our imaginations – especially mine. If we don't play our cards right, we'll be in science camp for the rest of the summer."

Jane followed me onto the porch. I was about to open the back door when she said it.

"But Cyd, what about the frogs ...?" Jane was standing on the exact spot two steps down from me. That was where Frogzilla had been when I... I couldn't say anything. I looked at my feet, then her face. I had to help those frogs.

Jane didn't have much luck with pets. It wasn't that long ago when her wiener-dog, Schnitzel, was body slammed by a truck on our street. All the neighborhood

34

kids rushed out to see its squished wiener-dog body. The adults stood around talking about boring things, like how accidents like that wouldn't happen if only people kept their dogs on a leash.

Then there was Jane's turtle, Slow Poke. She thought he would like to sun himself by the kitchen window, so she left him on the window ledge. Let's just say we could have had baked turtle for dinner, if we'd wanted to.

Jane still had her rabbit and Yin, her cat. Yin was an indoor cat so she wouldn't get run over, stepped on, baked, or come into contact with any other life-threatening forces.

We'd gone through a lot of pets.

A cat to make up for the wiener-dog, a bird to make up for the turtle, and a fish, to make up for the ... well, that's another story.

"Tomorrow we'll look up the license plate

number on the 'net and get the names of those people." It was the first smile I'd seen on Jane's face since yesterday. She followed me into the house.

Mom must have heard the back door slam shut because she yelled out from the living room. "Cynthia, Jane, come in and meet my colleagues. They're Canadian scientists; they just finished working at a university in Paris, France. Now they'll be working with me in the genetics department."

I was grimy from our ride. I wiped my hands on my cut-offs and shook hands with a tall thin woman.

"This is Dr. Rita Smalley," said Mom.

I started to giggle but soon realized that it wasn't a joke. Dr. Smalley was one of the tallest people I'd ever met. Can grown-ups be tall for their age? Dr. Smalley was wearing a long summer dress that made her look even taller. Her hands were big and crushed my fingers when she shook my hand. She smelled like cat food.

"And this is her husband, Dr. Bert Tallbot."

I thought this was also a joke, but my mom wasn't laughing at this either. It must really be his name. This guy was huge. He fit into his name like a hand in a glove. My own hand disappeared into his fist, which felt like raw pizza dough. In this heat, it felt like the sauce was on it as well.

He had a round face the size of a honeydew melon. His dark round eyes smiled at me. He was bald except for a few strands of hair that fell over his forehead. He brushed them back with his fingers as if he couldn't wait for his next haircut.

His body was the shape of a bowling pin, wide in the middle where his belt hitched up over his belly. He had on shorts and a Genetics Department Baseball Team T-shirt that read *The Gene Team*.

"Do you ever go to the lab with your mom?"

His voice was like a glass of super-sweet lemonade.

"Yeah, sure," I answered. I wanted to tell him about the neat glasses you get to wear in the ultraviolet room, but I stopped. Where had I heard that voice before?

Jane poked me in the ribs with her finger. That's one thing we didn't share. She had the boniest fingers.

Drops of sweat on my forehead turned to ice. *Go to the lab ... lab partner.* Was it him? And her? We hadn't got a good look at them yesterday, but that voice!

Everything moved in slow motion. Jane tugged at the sleeve of my T-shirt. Our eyes met. I saw the horrified look on my face reflected in her eyes. She looked as scared as I felt. I kept talking. I knew I was forming words, but I don't know what I said. I steadied my voice, even and neutral the way Nancy Drew did, but the sounds coming out of my mouth shook like a tremor before an earthquake.

Mom went to the kitchen and Tallbot and Smalley joined her. They chitchatted, made small talk as my mother called it, but I couldn't make out what they were saying. Yin brushed against my leg. The next thing I knew, Jane and I had backed out of the living room. We ran up the stairs to our bedroom.

"It's him," Jane slammed the door. "And her! The *animals*." Jane gasped for air and leaned against the door as if Dr. Tallbot was right behind us.

"Look, don't panic. There must be an explanation," I said. "Maybe it's not really them. Are we sure? I bet the thieves weren't even scientists, just thieves hired to steal things. Maybe it was a prank."

"Explanation? What explanation? What would two scientists be doing with an Empire Meats truck? They were stealing frogs. They work with Mom." Jane only raised her voice when she was upset.

I pretended to be rational. A list, that's rational. "Okay, on the one hand, we never saw their faces." I gasped between breaths. "On the other hand, we only heard their voices. On the third hand, wait a minute. There isn't a third hand."

I swung around fast to face Jane. "They said they'd have to keep their lab partner out of it. What are the chances that Mom is their lab partner? There must be a million scientists. We know they work for the genetics department, but not which lab." And I thought *Jane* was the freak-out twin.

I sat down and breathed deeply. I was out of breath. My mouth was dry. I couldn't speak, which was rare for me. I looked at Jane, waiting for a reaction. Was she going to cry? No, her eyes were like steel.

"We have to find out what they're up to and what the experiments are for," she said. "What did they mean when they said this plot could mean jail or riches for them? We need more info, the 411 on these two."

"Cynthia, Jane." called Mom. "Supper is ready."

"Stay cool. Don't let on that anything is wrong," I whispered.

We heard Bert Tallbot's laughter as we walked down the stairs.

****

I pushed the wieners around in my macaroni, hiding them underneath the cheesy bits and ketchup. Dr. Tallbot ate a steak my mom barbecued. He hacked the meat into chunks that were way too big for his mouth. Then he piled them with potatoes and shoved them into his mouth. His cheeks were stuffed to the breaking point as bits of potato squished out from between his lips. Jane stared at him. I nudged her in

41

the ribs.

Dr. Smalley hardly ate anything. She cut off a tiny piece of meat and then chewed it about a hundred times. Then she took a sip of water and started all over again.

Mom launched her interrogation.

"That's a lovely scent you're wearing, Rita. Where did you get it?"

"In France. It was made especially for me from a rare plant." Dr. Smalley sniffed her wrist.

Eau de cat food. I'm sure it will catch on.

Mom commented, "I haven't heard much about what you worked on in France. Are you continuing the work you started there?"

Smalley made a choking sound and coughed into her hand. She looked at Talbot. Neither of them answered. She held her knife like a scalpel and focused on cutting a piece of meat that was exactly one square inch.

Tallbot answered with his mouth full. What would Mom have to say about that? I stared at my plate so I wouldn't have to watch. He mumbled something about cancer research, cells, chromosomes, genes and DNA. As if we didn't hear enough about that from our parents.

"What about animals?" Jane asked. "Do you do research on animals like, I don't know, maybe mice or cats?" She went back to reload, then shot. "Or frogs?"

Dr. Tallbot stopped in mid-chew. His eyes locked on Jane. Then they switched to me.

"Jane likes animals, that's all. She has a lot of pets." I watched his eyes.

He finished chewing his mouthful and stared at me like he was drilling a hole in my head to see into my brain. After a moment, one eyebrow arched. That's so mystery-book-evil-villain, I thought.

"No, not animals, just canola." He swallowed hard.

"Speaking of animals," Mom said, "I heard there was a break-in yesterday at one of the university labs. I guess they got away with a few cages of animals. Since I was at work, the police want to interview me, just in case I saw or heard anything."

Drs. Tallbot and Smalley clenched their knives and forks and shot a quick glance at each other.

Oh yeah, it was them all right. Jane and I tried not to look at each other.

"Do the police have any leads?" Bert asked.

"No, they think it was university students playing a prank. I didn't see anything; it was in a lab on another floor and I was in that endless faculty meeting." Mom grinned.

Bert fake smiled, then he let out what seemed

like a sigh of relief, or maybe it was a burp. He loaded up his fork again, and changed the subject.

"Jane likes animals, you say. We have the cutest poodle, Seymour. He's a little furry puffball. You would love him." Dr. Tallbot's face lit up like he wasn't evil. He directed a smile at my mom. Then he eyeballed me.

"If you girls are interested in science, next time you're at the lab, drop by my station and I would be pleased to tell you about my research. Wouldn't I, Rita?"

His voice was as sweet as cotton candy, but his eyes never left me. Could he tell what I was thinking? Did he mean it or was this a trap?

Chapter Five
The Cheese Pie Man

Future blog entry: <u>Thin crust or deep dish – Friend or Foe</u>
<u>– you decide.</u>

"Okay, maybe we should tell her. But how?" I
rubbed my chin.

"Cyd. We witnessed a crime, for crying out
loud. The break-in, remember? Let's just tell her. Mom
would want us to. What is it she always says ... we'd be
doing our civic duty, whatever that means?"

"Mom said the break-in was on another floor,
so it's not her lab. And besides, what if Mom thinks it's

one of our mystery novel plots?" My voice wavered. I didn't want Jane to know I was worried.

We were in Control Central; that's what I called it, anyway. Jane called it Nancy Drew's Hideout.

It was, in fact, an enormous clothes closet built into our room. It was so big that we could climb up, using the shelves like a ladder, and sit on the top shelf. Yin, the cat, loved it up here and crawled all over me.

This is where we kept most of our spy toys. Like the invisible ink I bought from an ad in the back of a comic book. The ink wasn't invisible, but it was fun to think of how we could write that into one of our mysteries. We kept all our mystery novels up here and worked out our plots.

We weren't sketching out a fictional plot twist now. We had stumbled upon a real mystery and had to figure out what to do. In a few minutes, Mom would be home from work early to drive Bert Tallbot to the airport to pick up luggage they had shipped from France.

"Maybe we should start going to work with her every day. We'll tell her it's take-your-twin-daughters to-the-lab day," said Jane. "Then we can look for clues, and it will be extra security just in case."

"Yeah, but we don't know if she's in danger. We don't know what Rita and Bert are up to."

"That's a lot of 'don't knows,'" said Jane. "Why can't you agree with me for once?"

"You mean like, for always. You always think you're right." I shot back.

"You're bossing me."

Mom called, "Girls, girls, what's all this bickering about? Do you want to come to the airport or continue your quest for first prize in your international bicker fest?"

We stopped talking. I grinned. "Good one,

48

Mom. Can I use that line sometime, or do you have copyright on it?" We ambled down from the closet.

"Come on, let's go," Mom urged. "It's getting late."

We wanted another opportunity to observe Bert Tallbot, so we made up a story about wanting to go along for the ride to watch the airplanes land. We said it was our next favorite thing to do besides cycling out to the mall. Yeah, when we were five!

Mom waved us through the door. I took advantage of her jocular mood to slide in a clue-defining question.

"Mom, would you say Rita and Bert ..."

"That's Dr. Smalley and Dr. Tallbot to you."

"Yeah, yeah, Dr. and Dr. Would you say they're your lab partners.'"

"Well, they are lab partners to each other because they're working on the same research. And we all work for the genetics department…"

It's all an infinite world of possibilities and probabilities with Mom.

I pressed on, "But if you met someone would you say here's my lab partner Dr…" By this time we were at the front door and nearly ran splat into the one Dr. in question.

"Hello, girls."

It was him. "Hello, Dr. Tallbot," we answered in unison.

"Call me Bert," he said.

Fat chance I'd call a potentially evil scientist by his first name.

There wasn't much room in the back seat because Dr. Tallbot slid the front seat all the way back so he could fit in his legs. Jane and I squished on one side of the back seat and she kept puffing her cheeks out to look like the Cheese Pie Man. That was our new name for him, the Cheese Pie Man. We didn't even know what a cheese pie was, but that didn't matter. We liked the sound of the Cheese Pie Man. That's what his face looked like.

"Maybe we should call him L'homme tarte fromage," I whispered into Jane's ear and she had an attack of the giggles. I guess that's why we go to French immersion school. I don't know why we were having such a good time. After all, this man was somehow involved in a frog-napping plot, doing hush-hush experiments out of sight of the genetics department, and we didn't know if it would put our mom in harm's way.

I pinched Jane to make her stop laughing and mouthed the words: *This is serious.*

****

"Let's try to hang around. He might drop a hint or something. But not get too close." said Jane.

Mom and the Cheese Pie Man were having a nice chat with the people from the airline to locate his luggage. Jane and I staked out a place by the luggage carousel to keep an eye on him.

We pretended we were looking for the luggage with the most duct tape on it so Mom wouldn't suspect anything. People rushed to collect their bags and bumped into Jane and mr like we were in a computer game.

Turns out Dr. Tallbot's luggage was too big for the chute. He went to the baggage-claim area to pick it up.

"Probably all those suits he got at the Fat and Gigantic shop," I said.

"Hey, who's that guy Mom's talking to now?" asked Jane.

The man had the eyebrows of an owl and a moustache that looked like a handful of twigs tied together in the middle. He wasn't as tall as Mom, who was tall enough to reach the spice cupboard without the step stool.

"Doesn't she know the do-not-talk-to-strangers rule applies to adults as well?" Jane murmured.

We sashayed over and planted ourselves behind a pillar. We wanted to catch some of the conversation before they noticed us and stopped talking because we were kids.

The twiggy-mustached man said, "Let me introduce myself: Monsieur Camembert Oulette, Cam for short."

I'll say he was short. Jane and I looked at each other and mouthed, "Cheese Omelette" at the same time. That was his new name: Monsieur Cheese Omelette.

"I'm the owner of the new French restaurant. Enchante, madame." With that, Monsieur kissed our mom's hand. Yuck. Hand sanitizer anyone?

I overheard Mom say how refreshing it was to have some fine cuisine close to our neighborhood. I figured it meant that Mom was happy there was more to choose from than Chinese food and pizza.

By the time Dr. Tallbot came back pushing a trolley piled high with trunks, Mom had gone to the washroom. Omelette hugged him and kissed him on both cheeks.

"Wait a minute, how do they know each other? They're both new in town." My twin doesn't miss a detail.

"Well, I'm surprised his lips didn't sink into those quicksand cheeks of Tallbot's. They must know each other, but from where?" My stomach was tied up in more knots than my shoelace.

Omelette talked quickly. His voice squeaked. Not only did they know each other, but it looked like they were arguing. Jane and I moved in closer.

We only heard a few words. Cheese Omelette's face turned red. He gripped the lapels of Tallbot's jacket, which was quite a feat because the Cheese Pie Man towered over him. "I want to get my money's worth ... we signed a contract ... the only reason I came to this one-buggy town.... I don't want a repeat of last time. I need to smell the sweet smell of success." Cheese Omelette shook Dr. Tallbot with each sentence. People walked past them toward the luggage carousel and didn't seem to notice.

Jane hissed, "Contract! Wasn't that what gangsters did when they wanted to get rid of someone?"

"Jane, this isn't TV."

"*Get his money's worth.* Are they in business together at the French restaurant?"

I was busy being indignant. "What did he mean

about this being a one-buggy town?" Sure, this wasn't a big city, but the number-twelve bus ran one street over from our house, and I'd never seen a buggy.

Omelette let go of Tallbot's lapels, pulled out a handkerchief, and wiped off his hands.

The Cheese Pie Man shook a sausage-sized digit at Omelette. "Mark my words, the world of science will envy us. So much for health and safety regulations. Get me that herb and don't come to the lab."

They both took a quick look around. That's when Mom showed up.

"I see you've got your luggage," Mom said. "Mr. Oulette, do you know my esteemed colleague, Dr. Bert Tallbot?"

"Oh, Dr. Tallbot, yes, you do look familiar! Didn't we meet at a reception at the university in Paris? My restaurant provided the food." Mr. Oulette held his hand out and winked at Tallbot. The look on the

Cheese Pie Man's face went from mad to surprised.

"Yes, I remember now. What a coincidence." Tallbot shook Oulette's hand and winced. "Rita and I will have to drop by your restaurant. I understand you relocated here." The Cheese Pie Man pulled a snake smile.

"You can get reacquainted," declared Mom as she pointed Tallbot toward the exit of the airport. Tallbot inched the trolley of mammoth luggage towards the door.

"Yes, we look forward to spending some time together." Omelette shot the Cheese Pie Man the evil eye.

"Well, then you must both come for dinner," Mom called over her shoulder, as Tallbot struggled against the weight of the trunks. We tagged along behind.

Jane hit her forehead with the heel of her hand

"What a bunch of fibbers! That's just like Mom, inviting a frognapper to dinner."

I spun Jane to face me and grabbed her by the shoulders. "Forget about that now. What do a scientist and a restaurant owner have to do with each other? And why was Omelette so mad? I'm afraid our next blog entry might be: *French Restaurant Serves up Cheese Pie Man.*"

Chapter Six
Mom's the Word

Jane snatched my Nancy Drew book from me. "How can you sit there reading? Let's check the license plate of the van. We need to know why those two are in cahoots."

In cahoots means conspiring together secretly, as in, hand in glove. I'd looked it up ages ago. Every good detective needs to know what that means. The Cheese Pie Man and Omelette were certainly in cahoots.

"All right already, don't blow a gasket. It's not a crime for two people to talk to each other in the airport." I was sitting on my bed, pretending to read to take my mind off what we heard yesterday. I needed to suss out if Nancy Drew ever had the likes of the Cheese Pie Man and Omelette to deal with. I picked the last of the cat hair off my T-shirt, pretty much a full-time job with Yin, and joined Jane at the desk.

She fired up the laptop and surfed the 'net. I cleared some space beside her and brushed away the notes, the digital camera and the USB cable that was still there from our last blog entry. The headline was: *Bike Wheels Fly as Kids Leave School for the Last Time.* I uploaded a digital picture of my bike wheel spinning around. That was the most exciting thing going on in our neighborhood before the mystery.

"I'll see whose name it's registered under." Jane sounded efficient. "Here it is. It's under the name

Empire Meats, a company owned by Chez Oulette."

We both looked at each other. "Chez Oulette," I said. "That's the name of Mr. Oulette's restaurant. You know ... Cheese Omelette." The laptop made a whirling sound in the background. "Keep looking."

"There are two addresses. One looks like the address for the restaurant and the other looks like it's in the industrial part of town. Wait, I'll download this as evidence."

"That's great, sis. Now we know for sure that he's in on the stealing animals part. But why?" I jumped off the bed and paced back and forth. "What does a restaurant owner have to do with two scientists doing experiments on animals they stole? Science and food. Food and science. I'm just free-flowing here, Jane. Let's see. There's a rule at school: No food in the science lab – because it stinks, the lab, not the food. French restaurant, French fries. There's that guy who uses leftover French fry grease to fuel his car. That's like science. Ahhh, it doesn't make any sense."

"Cyd, you're on the wrong track. It's about the animals. Why would they do clandestine experiments on animals for a restaurant owner?"

Clandestine. Another really good mystery writer word. Very cloak and dagger.

"Maybe Omelette invented a new kind of omelette and wants a patent on it."

Jane flashed me one of Mom's trademark, patented exasperated looks.

"Okay, seriously, maybe he's an amateur scientist and he hired them to do some experiments. Oh, wait, I've got it. Maybe he's found a spice that cures the cold and he's mixed it up in a formula and wants to sell it. And he needs some real scientists to test it. You know, lab tests. Mom's always going on about how they have to test things to make sure they actually work."

"That could be it." Jane jotted it down in her notebook. Pencil in mouth, she chewed on the idea. "The Cheese Pie Man did say something about a herb. They would need the animals to test the formula before they test it on humans. But why all the sneaking around? I want to do one more search. Let's see: *Paris, universities, Tallbot* and *Smalley*. Mom said they worked in a university in Paris." Jane hit return.

I hovered over her. We waited for the search engine to come up with some links. In seconds, there were ten thousand listings. Most were Paris tourism sites. We scrolled down until we found sites with *Tallbot* and *Smalley*. There were a few listings; most were conferences at which the two had presented research papers.

"Here's something." Jane clicked on a link and waited for it to open. "It's a newspaper article, in French. Give me a minute to read it." She studied the article and then sucked in her breath. "Holy cow, Cyd, you are not going to believe this."

"What? Read it out loud!"

"Okay, the headline ... 'Scientists Kicked out of University, Research Halted.' It says that the two scientists, Bert Tallbot and Rita Smalley, were engaged in research that was deemed harmful to the population, both humans and animals."

Her eyes darted between the screen and me. I leaned in closer. "This is it, Cyd. We've discovered the mystery. This is big – *international* big. They're going to be in trouble now."

Jane scrolled down the article. "Let's see here... they kept going despite the fact that the guys who make the rules asked them to stop. Then something about putting greed before safety...It goes on to say that not all scientists are bad and that most research benefits humankind, blah, blah, blah."

I swung Jane's chair out of the way and looked at the article. "Does it say what their research was about?"

Jane swiveled back in front of the computer. "No, this looks like a follow-up article. There aren't a lot of details about the actual research." She scrolled down to the bottom. A picture of Drs. Smalley and Tallbot sneered back at her. She hit the print button and then closed out of the article. "So, now what do we do? I say we go straight to the police with this."

"Forget about the police, let's show this to Mom. She'll shut them down quicker then a sleepover past midnight." I plopped down on my bed.

"Yeah, she'll go tell the president of the university or something and it will all be out in the open and then we'll find out how Omelette's involved."

"Forget about Omelette, too. He's eggs on toast to us now. It's the scientists who are up to no good.

We've cracked our first case and we didn't even have to recycle the shells. High fives all around." Even Yin got an extra cuddle.

***

We spent the rest of the day killing time like it was fifth grade science class.

We were on Mom as soon as she got home, like Yin on an open can of cat treats.

"Mom, look at this." I shoved the printout of the article at her.

"Oh, great, the next edition of your electronic magazine. I'm dying to know what happened to those garbage cans. You know I'm your greatest fan." Mom yanked off her shoes and swung her workbag into the hall closet. "It looks more like a real newspaper every time."

I followed her to the living room. "No Mom, it's called a 'zine and it isn't our 'zine. We stopped doing a 'zine ages ago because they are so turn-of-the-century. We've got a blog now. That's short for an electronic weblog – get it? – *blog*? This isn't a 'zine and it's not off our blog." It was frustrating explaining technology to grown-ups.

"It's a newspaper article that I found on the 'net and printed out," Jane piped up. "It's about Tallbot and Smalley." She sounded like a hard-bitten detective already.

"It's all in French, glad to see you're using your French, give me a minute...." Mom's eyes sank into the article as she sank to the couch. The look on her face turned from happy to disappointed to mad in a nanosecond. Well, maybe two nanoseconds.

"Oh, now you girls have gone too far. I turned a blind eye about the article titled: *Snooper Pooper – who's not scooping up after their dog?* Which was clearly aimed at our neighbor down the street. And the one with the title: *Science Teacher Wouldn't Know DNA if it Dripped Out of his Nose and Slithered down to Land on his Genes.* But this is taking it too far. This is slandering the reputation of two scientists you met once. Destroy this and all the copies you have. I'm disappointed in you girls. I thought you'd be able to handle unstructured time."

We stood there, stunned, like kids in first grade. The force of her anger was like walking into a strong wind.

"No, really Mom, it's an article from a newspaper in France. We didn't make it up," Jane said.

"I could expect as much from you Cyd, with all your plots and subplots, but not you, Jane. I don't want to hear any more of this."

Mom stormed into the kitchen, leaving us there holding the only evidence we had. If anyone would have believed us, I thought it would be Mom.

We ate cold chicken in silence. Next blog entry title could have been: *Two Hard-Boiled Detectives get Fried by Mother.* But Jane and I headed to Control Central right after dinner.

I don't know any detectives who would let a little cold shoulder stop them from solving a crime against humanity. And frogs.

Chapter Seven
The Plant Vault

"Get your digital camera out and take a picture of that block of cheese in the fridge," commanded Jane.

"Do you have sunstroke? Here. Take a swig of water"

It was the next day. We were in the back yard getting some sun – or absorbing Vitamin D as my mom called it. We needed a plan and fast. I remembered the tone of Omelette's voice and the intensity of the

Cheese Pie Man's stare. But Jane wasn't making sense.

"So what if Mom doesn't believe us? We know what we saw." Jane had that look of determination on her face I only saw when she talked about animals. She sat there with the laptop on her knees, her notebook beside her and a pencil clasped in hand. Yin stared at me through the blades of grass like she was a lion on safari.

"We need to blog about this. Mom clearly doesn't read our blog or even know what century this is – remember when she asked how to put the film into the digital camera? We need more clues. We can't wait for Mom to believe us."

Jane was on fire now. Her fingers flew across the keyboard like dandelion fluff flew across the neighborhood in the spring.

"We'll put our blog entries up and see if our friends give us any leads to follow. They won't know who we're talking about and will think the Cheese Pie Man and Omelette are fictional characters."

"Yeah, great idea." I grabbed the digital and headed toward the house. Hopefully there would be a bit of mold on the cheese.

I was back. I opened up the blog from where it was bookmarked, and the cute digital picture I uploaded of Jane and me appeared in the corner. I hooked the cable from the digital camera into the laptop and downloaded the picture to my picture file. Then I uploaded it to the blog entry Jane had written. A big block of cheese next to the entry title:

***

Blog Entry: _The proof isn't always in the pudding; sometimes it's in the Cheese Omelette._

Animals stolen from a university lab in the heat of a summer day. The only evidence is a slab of cheese pie followed by a helping of cheese omelette. Two scientists

argue over which animals to steal and talk about formulas. Why now, why frogs and why cheese...?

***

I read it twice, scratched my head and found a mosquito bite. I tried to be positive, not sarcastic. "That's great, Jane. It's a little cryptic, more like Egyptian hieroglyphics. But it's good. Why don't we write it like a plot line? Write it how it's happening *now*?"

"Just because Mom doesn't read our blog doesn't mean other people who know her don't. Like the parents of our friends; teachers; neighbours; Dad in England. If she gets tipped off that we're writing about the scientists it will be science camp for us all summer."

"Yeah, you're right," I agreed. "Let's get back to the evidence and clues. If we could only figure out the link between the Cheese Pie Man and Omelette. "

"No, first we need to find out what the research was about. Then they'll listen." Jane grabbed her notebook and started writing in point form. She talked at the same pace as she scribbled:

"#1: Omelette said he didn't want a repeat of what happened in France.

"#2: On the day of the robbery, Smalley said the experiment would be the difference between riches or jail.

"#3..." Jane's voice trailed off in frustration. "There's no #3, Cyd. Nobody said anything about the frogs or what the formula would be used for."

Jane slammed the notebook shut. "We are the only witnesses."

"If we can figure out why they need all those animals, then we'll know what the experiment is about. We need a plan." I thought for a moment about the plans in my favorite Nancy Drew books as I reached down to scratch behind Yin's ears. The old versions, written when our mom was young, were good. But the new versions were a lot cooler. Nancy had a cell phone and drank lattes.

I rubbed my chin. "Okay, we're going over to the lab at lunch to look for clues. It's a nice day. Everyone will be in the park eating," I said in my best amateur detective voice. "Then if we don't have any luck, we'll follow up on the license plate lead."

"But what if Mom is eating lunch in her office?" Jane objected. "She'll suspect something."

"Mom hates eating around all the radiation and chemicals and stuff. I made her lunch this morning and I packed the cold chicken and broccoli from last night. You know what that means. Right now she's experimenting on broccoli. She never eats the vegetable she's experimenting on. So, when Mom realizes that there's broccoli in her lunch, she'll probably grab a bagel and eat in the park." I sounded like a detective already.

We went inside to pack up our backpacks. Along with notebook, pencils....

I added, "Besides, if Mom is there, we'll ask what she's working on and pretend to be interested in science and genetics and stuff."

Every now and then, we'd pull an article off the web about the cloning of the woolly mammoth and show it to our parents, just to throw them a bone. A big woolly mammoth bone.

"She loved our idea for a mystery novel where the character solved a mystery at a science conference. We called it *The Case of the Missing Cell,* or something like that. Let's go," said Jane.

"Wait. We need a special bird call, like Nancy Drew has with Bess and George."

"Okay, but let's make it a cat meow. It will be like

the meow Yin makes when she wants attention." Jane gave a demonstration and Yin perked up her ears.

"All her meows are like that," I said, heading for the door. I grabbed the latest mystery book I was reading and put it in my backpack, just in case it came in handy.

****

Before we got into Mom's lab we had to get past the security guard. He was an old guy who knew us because we had come to the lab before with Mom. But she wasn't expecting us today. She usually gave the guard a list of visitors and he would be ready with a nametag that read, *I'm visiting a Radiation Zone.* Jane thought Mom should get one of those for my half of our room. Mom didn't think that was funny.

Jane always knew where everything was, including some old passes that we'd kept as souvenirs. We put them on in case we got caught.

Turned out we didn't need them.

The guard was down the hallway, making arm movements like he was landing a plane, giving directions to a student. Since it was summer, the university was nearly empty. We walked in. No problem.

We popped into Mom's office, where she prepared her university lectures. She wasn't there. We went into the lab to make sure she wasn't at her lab station. The lab was empty. I was right. Mom was out for lunch.

The lab stank like a hospital. Mega-clean, like antiseptic. A microscope stood ready at every workstation with rows and rows of test tubes. There were signs everywhere that read *Radiation Zone, Ultraviolet light - Eye Protection Must be Worn* and, *Your mother doesn't work here, so clean up after yourself!*

Well, that sign wasn't true. Our mother did work here, but we weren't about to mess up anything.

"What do we do first?" Jane asked.

"Look for clues, what else? And stop holding on to my shirt."

Jane let go and pulled her notebook and pencil out of her backpack.

We checked out each lab station. "That looks like Dr. Tallbot's over there." There was a picture of Seymour the French poodle. The Cheese Pie Man told me about him the other night at our house, like I was the one crazy about animals and not Jane. It was pinned up beside a poster of a cell that read, *Variety is the Splice of Life.* That passes for a joke in a science lab.

"There's nothing here," I said. The lab was spotless, almost as if the Cheese Pie Man hadn't done any work all morning. Maybe he wasn't guilty of a crime. Maybe he was only guilty of goofing off.

"Nancy would observe everything," Jane pointed out.

79

We scanned his lab station. There was a microscope, a Bunsen burner and an overhead light. Safety goggles lay on their side. Jane jotted some notes down, *Time: Lunch, Location: Cheese Pie Man's lab station. Lab station clean. No sign of activity,* she wrote. I could hear the clock tick on the wall. Jane broke the silence. "Let's look for clues in the vault."

My stomach clenched like Yin's claws around a cat toy. The vault, as Jane called it, was down the hall from the lab. It was a greenroom that had controlled light and heat. The size of a meat locker, it was where they grew plants and studied them at different stages of growth. It all had to do with DNA and genetics and blah, blah, blah, like we cared. Mom said DNA were the three most important letters in the universe, but to Jane and me, *DVD* were the three most important letters in the entire universe.

The green room did look like a vault, though.

80

It had a big bank-vault door. I always stayed near the door in case it shut. Jane liked the plant vault because Mom only experimented on plants. The shelves held rows and rows of plants that all looked the same. The air sagged with humidity. Grow lights made the plant vault hot.

"What exactly are we looking for, Jane?"

My sister's notebook was at the ready. She peered under leaves. I rubbed my hands together. My palms stuck with sweat. I was afraid someone would come back, see the door open and shut it. Then we'd never get out. We'd start to grow vines from our hair, tree branches from our arms, and roots from our runners.

"I don't know ... something to do with the animals that were stolen. Maybe we should look for fingerprints."

"On plant leaves? Maybe it would be easier to

look for signs of photosynthesis. Maybe it wasn't the butler. Maybe the sun was to blame all along."

"Can't you be serious for once? This may be our only chance to look for clues."

We heard a voice outside the plant vault. My back stiffened. It was *his* voice. It came from the lab. "Let's get out of here," I whispered. "That's Tallbot. Mom will be back soon."

We snuck back to the door of the lab and pretended to read a poster in the hallway, about genetic coding, in case anyone came by. The chemical smell tingled up my nose. A sneeze threatened like a mid-summer thunderstorm. I could hear the elevator ding at different floors. It wouldn't be long now before everyone came back from lunch. We didn't have much time.

We heard Tallbot speak. "Mr. Oulette, I will have the results for you as soon as possible. These things take time. I am a scientist after all, not a baker. I cannot cook up a formula just like that. This is a creation. It takes time. You just worry about your part."

Tallbot had to be on the phone because we couldn't hear Mr. Oulette's voice. Jane flipped open her notebook and wrote down what the Cheese Pie Man was saying. Hmmm ... maybe I'd make a detective out of her yet.

I leaned closer to the door and listened just like any good detective would have done. My nose tickled. I rubbed it.

"Okay, I promise you. My wife and I will go to the warehouse tomorrow – the warehouse you rented for us – but it might not work. It's fine for storing the animals, but we can't conduct the experiments there. Frogs are delicate creatures. I have to do the experiment just right, under certain conditions."

Long pause, nose itchy. I must not sneeze.

"Yes, yes, we will see what we can do. Then we must talk about the money. I want it in cash and I want a cut of the profits. I'm not doing this for the good of the frog kingdom, you know." He cackled.

Another pause. Nose scrunched up. I held back on the sneeze.

"Oh, and get me some more frogs. We will be using quite a few before we are finished. I don't care how you get them; we can't steal anymore. It's too risky. Go to a pet store or something, buy them off of a kid, get them out of the lake. I don't care!" The Cheese Pie Man let out an exasperated breath.

The sound of his voice sent shivers to my head, like an ice-cream brain freeze. I couldn't hold back the sneeze. It burst out. This one would have won me the international sneezing contest in a jiffy. Jane let out a squeal. I cupped my hand over her mouth.

"Wait a minute ... there was a noise in the

hallway," Tallbot said. "I'd better go check it out." I heard him slam down the phone.

Jane and I shot a glance at each other and ran for the elevator. We pressed the button, and then decided the stairs would be faster. That's the great thing about being a twin; you save a lot of time talking since you already know what the other is thinking.

"That was a close one," Jane puffed. Ten flights of stairs was a long way to run even if it was down.

"If he had seen us ...." I took a deep breath. It felt good to breathe fresh air and not the smelly lab air that Tallbot breathed. I shooed away a swarm of mosquitoes that buzzed by my ear.

"Looks like we're going on a bike trip to the warehouse tomorrow," I panted. "It's the only way we'll find out what's going on."

Future blog title: <u>Colossal Number of Mosquitoes isn't the only Mystery in Town.</u>

Chapter Eight
Frogstorm

"I just want to doublecheck the address." Jane was deep in cyberspace.

I packed our lunch. It was going to be a long bike ride. I sighed, "Nancy Drew had a car."

"Yeah, but it was a convertible. Wouldn't be good on a day like today."

I peered out the window. The sky threatened rain.

"That's just in the older books; in the newer

books she has a hybrid." Way to save the environment, Nancy.

We had two bikes. "Let's just go. It's out by Fish Fry Park. We used to go there for picnics when we were kids."

"No, it's near the Wildwood Bird Sanctuary. Remember, Mom and Dad got us up at dawn for a bird watching trip? There are some industrial buildings around there. I downloaded a bike map of the city. We can take the paths most of the way and not be on the main streets, like we promised Mom."

We'd told Mom we were going on a bike ride to the nature reserve just past the mall. We hadn't even left and already Jane felt guilty.

"Check the blog to see if anyone commented on the last entry."

Jane pulled up the bookmark of our blog. "One comment." She clicked on it. It flashed on the screen.

"Hey it's from Dakota." Dakota was my lab partner in science class. Jane was useless as a partner. If a science project included animals, Jane was prone to pulling a Gandhi and doing the whole passive-resistance thing.

I said, "Dakota's in Paris with her parents and she promised she'd check in on the blog over the summer. I'll read out her comment."

***

Response to blog entry: <u>The proof isn't always in the pudding ...</u>

Is there a big fork?

Frogs are lab experiments

Will the omelette fry?

P.S. How's Yin, the Queen of the Hairballs?

Or wait, this one's better: It's Hairball City and she's the mayor.

***

88

"Is she kidding?" Jane looked fit to be tied.

"It's a Haiku. You know, a Japanese poem, three lines. The first line has five syllables, the second has seven, then five."

"Yeah, I know what a Haiku is, Cyd. You don't have to explain it to me. What is she talking about?"

In addition to being my lab partner, Dakota and I liked to play word games and write poems. "*Big fork.* Hmm. Maybe she means, is there a big cheese? You know, like a ringleader. Will the omelette fry? Have to think on that one.

"The middle line is about how frogs are good for lab experiments because they've been experimenting on frogs for centuries. But you'd know that if you'd ever experimented on one. "

The look Jane glared at me was a cross between anger and tears. I figured *I'd* be in tears if I didn't zip it.

"Just because they've been experimenting on frogs for centuries doesn't mean it's the right thing to do."

We agreed to use the bike ride to think about Dakota's comments. Finally, on the road, I looked up at the sky. It glared down at me. A dark bluish-grey sky had replaced the clouds and I could smell rain in the air. Fine time for a summer storm.

We'd been riding for what seemed like hours. It was time for a snack. We pulled over and ate the peanut butter and jam sandwiches we'd packed. "What do we do when we find the animals there?" I asked. A couple of wasps dive-bombed for our food.

"I don't know. Take notes, I guess. We want to find out what is going on with the frogs. I sure hope the Cheese Pie Man doesn't throw a net over us and trap us in his lair which turns out to be a cave, and we have to dig our way out with a bone from a skeleton," said Jane.

And I was supposed to be the one with the wild imagination. I stopped chewing in mid-bite. "That sounds like a great plot line for a case of The Cyd Files, but stuff like that doesn't happen in real life."

Jane looked relieved. "You mean, The Jane Files." She grinned and finished her sandwich. We got back on the road.

"Okay, the C&J Files," I shouted into the wind.

After an hour of pedaling hard against the wind, we reached the industrial part of town. Most of the buildings were new.

"According to the map, it's that one." Jane pointed at a run-down old warehouse.

We hid our bikes behind some bushes, and then went around the back where we found a window. I threw my backpack on the grass. Drops of rain plunked against my face as I wiped the grime off the window

91

and peered in. There were cages of animals, but no Tallbot and Smalley.

"Let's go in." Jane headed for the door.

"Wait a minute, that's breaking and entering. That's illegal."

"Cyd, did you think we'd come all this way and not go in? This is about saving animals, and maybe catching criminals. Nancy Drew breaks into places. She never waits for Chief McGuinness to get a search warrant."

"We don't even know if they committed a crime," I muttered. Boy, when did Jane get so brave? I grabbed the backpack and followed, but kept an eye out the whole time.

The doorknob wouldn't budge when Jane turned it. She shoved her shoulder against the door and pushed. It creaked open. We crept into the warehouse. It was more like a barn with a high ceiling and beams. Dust inched up my nose. On one side was a pile of lumber and logs. The walls shuddered against the howling wind.

The warehouse was dim inside; a little light seeped through the grimy windows, but it wasn't so dark that we couldn't see everything. Tables, like the ones in a community hall, held rows and rows of cages filled with animals.

The animals cowered.

There was an ancient bathtub filled with frogs. The wind died down and the sound of their croaking filled the warehouse.

Jane took one look, saw that the frogs were okay, and ran straight for the cages with the cats. She opened one of the cages and picked up a cat. "Look, this one likes me." She cuddled it.

"Jane, don't mess with anything. They'll know we've been here. Let's just look, get some clues, and get out of here." Thunder clapped. I flinched at the noise. A streak of lightning lit up the warehouse. Rain hammered against the windows. My hands shook, but I got out my notebook and looked around.

There were cages of mice and cats – arch-enemies of the animal kingdom. How smart is that? Dust everywhere, not at all like Mom's lab. There was a table near the window. A special light was set up and there were rows and rows of test tubes. A different color of liquid filled each vial. That area was spotless.

If only Mom were here, she'd know what was going on. I reached for a vial. I heard the door rattle, and then I heard the voices of Bert Tallbot and Rita Smalley. My stomach lurched. Jane swung around and the cat bolted. We ran for the pile of lumber and logs and hid behind it. There was no need for our special cat meow.

"It's a bear of a day," said the Cheese Pie Man,

94

as he shook his rain-drenched body. He left a small puddle around himself. "I heard that if you run in the rain, you get one-third fewer drops on you than if you walk in the rain. Isn't that interesting?"

"And folklore has it that frogs increase their croaking just before a storm," added Dr. Smalley.

A frog croaked as if to confirm her theory. Scientists, what a bunch.

Jane whispered. "What if they notice the cat is missing? What about our footprints?"

"Shh. As long as they don't notice the cat's cage is empty, we'll be fine. We'll wait here until they leave, and then we'll get out."

"Hey, what's this?" shouted Rita. She rushed for the open cage. "One of the cats is gone." She whirled around, as if she expected someone to sneak up on her.

We didn't have to worry. The rain dripped off

their bodies and they took the same path to the cages that we had, so their muddy boots smudged over our footprints.

"Someone's been in here," Dr. Smalley shouted.

Jane whimpered. Sweat mingled with the rain on my forehead. It felt like my hair was crying.

"I must have left that cage door open last night," Dr. Tallbot said. "It doesn't matter if we lose one cat. Don't worry about it; no one has used this old warehouse in years."

Jane squeezed my hand. I held my breath. It was darker now because of the storm. The frogs croaked louder.

"Look, there's the cat." Tallbot pointed to the beams. He walked toward Smalley, and his face went all business. "Let's get to work. We don't want to be here all night in this storm."

Rita shrugged. Jane and I breathed again. We peered through the gaps in the pile of lumber and logs and watched as the two doctors went to the lab station and prepared the syringes.

"Once we see how the formula reacts on mammals, we can inject the frogs," said Tallbot. "We don't want a repeat of last time, do we now, my sweet?"

I felt Jane tense up beside me. Please don't do anything stupid, I telepathically communicated twin to twin.

Rita Smalley explained, "We were so close last time. We can't do the frog experiments here. We don't have time to clean it and make it into a lab. We need a different environment. The humidity level needs to be just right so the frogs will survive after we inject them."

She stuck the syringe into a vial and pulled the

97

plunger. She motioned to the bathtub filled with frogs. "They're fine here now, but we'll need a bigger place, especially when the formula starts working." She smirked.

"When we're at the lab tomorrow night, let's look around. Maybe we can hide them there," said Tallbot.

Smalley rolled her eyes back in her head. "Oh, that would be great. You've already given our lab partner enough evidence to sink a test tube cleaner. If she finds out about the plan, it'll all be over. Here, hold this." Smalley slapped the syringe into his hand.

"She won't find out. She's too wrapped up in her own research. She hasn't a clue. And if she does, we'll just take care of her."

"Well, stop being so friendly to her and her snoopy kids." Smalley opened a cage and pulled out a cat. She shoved it at Tallbot. He handed the syringe back. He held the cat in one big hand, cradled it close to his body and stroked its back.

The palms of my hands sweated and the backs of my legs ached from crouching so long. My legs cramped up. I needed to stretch. Jane started to whimper again. Dust was getting up my nose and I felt a sneeze coming on. Some pair of super detectives we made. How were we going to get out of this warehouse?

Dr. Smalley held up the syringe and tapped it with the back of her finger just like a doctor does before a vaccination. Then she lightly pressed in the plunger and a few drops of formula squirted out. She handed the needle back to Tallbot. I saw some movement on the rafters and looked up. The cat Jane had let out walked across the beams. Thunder cracked. That cat let out a howl, leaped down and landed on the table with the vials. The table shook and I heard the sound of test tubes clinking together. The test tubes cascaded

99

off the table and the warehouse filled with the sound of glass breaking. Tallbot and Smalley gasped.

Then, silence.

The cat hopped down and scooted toward us. I willed myself to become invisible; it didn't work, of course, so I just kept still.

"The experiment, the vials, all ruined with one pounce of a cat." Tallbot twirled around with the cat he held out in one hand and the syringe in the other. "Ruined, all ruined."

"We'll have to start from scratch with the formula," Smalley fumed.

Tallbot dropped the cat he had planned to inject, and rushed toward the pile of lumber. He held the needle high. "That cat, that troublemaker, will be the first experiment."

The cat had found us and was cuddled up on my lap, of all places. As Jane shifted to take a protective stance over the cat and me, she knocked a log out of place.

Tallbot heard the wood move. He stopped dead in his tracks of rainwater and mud. He held the needle in front of his body like it was a weapon.

Cold sweat dripped down my forehead even though it was hot in the warehouse. What would he do when he found us? Thunder crashed and the frogs croaked. Tallbot grabbed at the lumber with his free hand and threw it piece by piece behind him. He was as mad as a hornet.

Jane shoved a log out from the bottom of the pile. It was now in the path of the Cheese Pie Man. In his rage he didn't see it and tripped. It was like watching a tree fall. He tried to stop himself and toppled over a few more logs on the way down. He landed on his stomach. When Tallbot scrambled to sit up, the syringe was sticking out of his chest.

"Yikes, that hurts," Tallbot yelled. "Pull it out, pull it out!"

His fingers shook as he tried to pull it out. He fumbled and pressed in the plunger. The Cheese Pie Man stumbled to his knees and hoisted himself up by grabbing onto the pile of wood.

Our hiding place was being destroyed one log at a time. We crouched lower so they couldn't see us. I scouted out another exit. The only way out was through the door or a window.

He whirled around screaming and ran to Smalley.

She pulled out the needle.

"Oh, no! Not the formula. What if it ...?"

They looked at each other, appearing dumbfounded. Neither moved for a moment. Tallbot wiped his hand on his shirt, as if he could wipe off some of the formula.

"Do we still have the formula for the antidote?" he yelled.

"No, I destroyed all my notes in France. Let's get you home. I can wash it out properly there."

They ran out and the door flapped in the wind.

"All right!" Jane shouted. She jumped up from behind the lumber. "Cats rule." She did a little happy dance. I heard a car drive off in the rain.

"You rule," I congratulated Jane. I never thought I'd see you hurt anyone. You toppled him. The Cheese Pie Man fell faster than a house of cards."

"That's one less animal he'll harm." The cat hightailed it back up to the rafters.

"Let's get out of here." I grabbed Jane and headed for the door.

We had to race to get home before Mom got back from work. At least the rain and wind were at our backs.

Where were Nancy Drew and her hybrid car when you need them?

My legs felt numb by the time we got home. Mom said we looked like drenched gophers. I had a long, hot bubblebath; Yin sat on the side of the tub and batted the bubbles with her paw. I scratched, under the water, at a new crop of mosquito bites on the back of my legs. Why were there so many mosquitoes this year? It had been a dry spring.

After all that, we had a few more clues but still didn't know what the villains' plan was. Like Nancy Drew says, you have to throw out a lot of lines before you catch a scientist bio-chemically altering frogs. Okay, Nancy probably never said that, but she should have. The only thing we knew was that Tallbot and Smalley would be visiting the lab the next night. And so would we.

Chapter Nine
A Frog Symphony

"How long are we going to wait here?"

Jane nudged me out of my daydream. Those bony fingers again. We were in the hallway, spying on Mom. Well, spying isn't the right word; let's just say we were waiting for the right moment. Jane was going to pretend to help Mom with supper and grill her for information about Dr. Tallbot's experiment.

Mom was busy cutting carrots in the kitchen. She sliced them so thin that she could probably count the number of cells in each slice. It looked like she was going to put the slices under her microscope instead of in the casserole.

"Okay, okay. Go on." Then I caught a glimpse of Jane's hands. Ketchup-flavoured potato chip crumbs covered them.

"Wait, look at your hands. You know Mom hates it when we come into her lab, er, kitchen with dirty hands," I said.

"I'll wash them when I rinse out the recycling."

Mom and Dad were old-school when it came to recycling. They didn't believe it was important. Jane and I knew better – global warming, polar bears, and receding ice caps – we were in charge of the recycling.

"No, I'll go." I had offered to pump Mom for clues. After all, I'd read enough mystery novels to know all the right questions to ask.

"No. You'll give us away." Jane elbowed past me.

Holy cow, bony elbows too.

"Mom, what are the Cheese Pie Man, I mean Dr. Tallbot, and Dr. Smalley working on in the lab?"

"Why Jane, it's nice that you're finally taking an interest in genetics. Hand me the milk from the fridge will you?"

"Well, I've been thinking about what you said about DNA being the three most important letters in the universe. And what with you and Dad being scientists, I thought..."

Jane handed Mom the milk jug and I could see the set of red fingerprints she left. Good thing identical twins don't have identical sets of fingerprints or I'd be blamed for sure. When Mom drained the last of the milk into her casserole, Jane swished it with water, squished it, and put it in the recycling box.

Come on Jane, I thought, get on with it. I would have had the mystery solved and the Cheese Pie Man in jail by now.

Mom said, "I think they're continuing some work they started in France. It's probably cancer research, like what I'm working on. They won't talk about their work in a lot of detail until the results have been published."

"Does it have anything to do with experiments on animals, like, let's say, cats and mice? Does it have anything to do with viruses?" Jane sped up. "We learned about viruses in school, especially the subterranean flu virus. Can a person create a virus? Then put it into the drinking water somehow, so everyone will get sick?"

"Scientists are professional and ethical; they would never think to do that. Where would you get that idea? You're more likely to get a virus from sneezing into your hands than through the water supply. "

I was still in the hallway, but I knew that Jane had blown it. She'd blurted out the whole virus in the water theory, and we didn't even know if that was true, even with the new clues we had. Now she wouldn't get any more scientific stuff out of Mom.

"Really, Jane, you must be watching those late night horror movies again with Cynthia. Now go and wash up. Dinner will be ready in twenty minutes."

"One more thing. Would people be working in the lab at night?"

"Not normally, honey. Not unless they had a big deadline to meet."

Deadline! I didn't like any word with dead in it when we were talking about the Cheese Pie Man. Jane wiped the last of the red stain off her hands on a dish towel and turned to look at me. She gave me her Let's-meet-in-Control-Central look. We needed a plan.

I was way ahead of her.

****

Blog Entry: <u>*Itchy Much? What's the buzz on all these mosquitoes?*</u>

I itch therefore I scratch,

My kingdom for some bug spray,

Why all the mosquitoes?

****

I posted my latest blog entry and was just about to upload a picture of a mosquito sucking blood from an arm when Mom popped her head in.

"Okay girls, I'll be back when the concert is over."

This was part of my plan. Mom liked to go to classical guitar concerts with her friends when Dad was out of town. She used to drag Jane and me along when we were little, but we had a habit of yawning loudly during what she called the best parts.

I heard the door shut. Mom was gone.

"Okay, we only have a few hours until Mom's back. Plus, we don't know what time they lock the building. We have to get in, see if the Cheese Pie Man and Rita have set up a secret lab for their experiments, and get out. Let's go, Cyd."

"So, they *did* mean Mom when they talked about their lab partner, because they mentioned her kids."

"Other scientists have kids," pointed out Jane.

"Yeah, but not snoopy kids. They said 'and her snoopy kids.' We're the snoopiest kids around."

The streetlights flickered on. It was strange to ride our bikes at night.

One thing was for sure, this had become more than just a plot for the Cyd and Jane Files. But I was worried about Jane. This whole frog thing was taking over her life. She kidded herself when she said she was over the death of her frog. For one thing, she didn't even say anything about my chipped reflector light. Usually that would be enough for her to call off a night raid to the lab.

Swarms of mosquitoes floated in the air. I brushed one swarm away from my ears and ducked to miss the next one.

We chanced that the building would still be open. The night security guard must have been on his rounds because he wasn't there. The elevator cables creaked and jolted. The elevator was creepy dark but a crack of light seeped in as it passed each floor. It seemed to take forever.

We first heard the noise when the elevator doors slid open. A dim light from Mom's lab cast a thin shadow into the hall. It wasn't voices, but the sound of frogs. Frogs croaking. Lots of frogs. We scurried to a spot by the bulletin board and listened outside the door. It was halfway open.

"There must be a hundred frogs in there," Jane whispered. I shushed her. The noise echoed into the hallway and bounced off the concrete walls. It was like an amphibian amphitheatre. So much for a secret lab!

Then we heard–

"Mr. Oulette, there was no need for you to come here tonight. I told you we would work on the experiment and we are."

It was the all-too-familiar sound of Cheese Pie Man's voice. In my mind, I saw the inside of his fridge stocked with loads of cheese and empty pie shells. I gave myself a shake. *Stay alert; we could get some great clues out of this.* I caught a glimpse of the Cheese Pie Man when he walked into view. His clothes looked too tight. Was he bigger than the last time I saw him? His science goggles perched on his forehead like an extra set of buggy eyes.

"We are scientists," came Rita Smalley's voice.

"We need peace and quiet to perfect the formula. We *don't* need you hovering over us like this. You have to trust us."

She walked into view holding a flask of green liquid. Frog juice? Yuck.

The frogs seemed to croak in unison. It was like a symphony of swamp noises. I thought of Mom at her concert. I heard the sound of the elevator door closing behind us and I felt Jane's hot breath on my neck.

I looked for the stairwell, just in case. We crouched closer to the door. My sneakers squeaked. I scratched a mosquito bite on my arm.

Oulette whined, "Listen Tallbot, while you are doing your little experiment, the clock ticks and more money is spent. You say that your lab partners have not caught on. How do you know that? This deal was supposed to make me money and now I am spending, spending, spending. What about safety? How do you

114

know it won't affect the people?" His voice hit a high note. Then it softened and escaped like the air from a balloon. "I don't want the same problems we had in France."

"Don't talk to me about France." Tallbot spat back. "We were so close in France. If only my nosy co-workers hadn't alerted the government people who make the rules!" He shook his hands in front of his face and then slowed his breathing down, calming himself. "None of this would have happened if they had made me Head Scientist, the Supreme Scientist of the Science Department, as they should have. I deserved it. Then I wouldn't have bothered with this. But now, I will take over the world of science. I will show all of them..."

"There, there Bert." Smalley patted his shoulder like she was comforting a kid.

Jane and I exchanged confused glances.

Tallbot got himself back together and pointed

a stubby finger at Oulette. "You leave the science to me and I'll leave the cooking to you. We are injecting the frogs tonight with the first formula. One week! You will see. If there are no results we will give you your money back and stop the experiments. You just keep me supplied with the herb from your village." Tallbot sounded like he meant it.

He and Smalley turned their backs on Oulette and went back to work. The air was thick with tension and the sound of frogs.

Oulette looked lost. I figured he would leave soon, but the only exit was the door we were standing beside. We had to make ourselves as scarce as Yin did when we discovered one of her hairballs.

I tapped on Jane's shoulder to signal that we should vamoose. She was as tense as a stretched elastic. *Don't freak out,* I telecommunicated twin-to-twin. I hoped she wouldn't make any sudden moves. I heard a thud, then another and then a pencil rolling on the floor. It wasn't coming from the lab. It was Jane. She had dropped her notebook, the mystery book, and her pencil. She jumped up and stood there stunned, like a frightened twin statue. I got up. "Don't worry, they'll never hear that over the frogs, but we need to get out of here."

"What was that? Someone must have followed you, Oulette. I knew it was a bad idea for you to come here."

My knees shook. I took one look at Jane. We grabbed the notebook, the book, chased the pencil halfway down the hall, and ran. Light shone from the plant vault. I shoved Jane in, followed her, and pulled the door handle shut. I heard their footsteps as they rounded the corner. The air was heavy, like in the tropical plant house on the top floor of the building, with its warm grow lights. I tried not to breathe. I clamped my hand over Jane's mouth because I wasn't sure if whimpers or screams would come out.

We heard voices.

"It was nothing," Rita said. "We've got each other spooked. Let's jab those hoppers and get out of here. We've got to stash the formula until next week."

"Right. Oulette, leave now before anyone sees you."

"Soon I will go back to France and forget the whole deal." We heard his footsteps as he stormed off. I took my hand from Jane's mouth. She gulped in air.

"Good. Now they'll go back to the lab and we can leave," I whispered. Sweat dribbled down my forehead. The knot in my stomach was beginning to loosen. I couldn't wait to get out of there.

"What are you doing?" Rita Smalley asked.

"Just locking the plant vault." Tallbot replied.

"It's supposed to be locked when we leave for the day."

Tallbot put on the latch. The padlock clicked into place. The key turned in the lock. Jane's nails bit into my arm. My eyes smarted from the sweat. Footsteps got fainter. How much air could there possibly be? We had to be home soon or Mom would notice we were gone. I gasped and wiped my face with my T-shirt. Silent tears streamed down Jane's cheeks.

Chapter Ten
Enormous Amphibians

"No, wait, sweetie. We had better leave it unlocked. What if someone notices tomorrow that it's locked? They may suspect we were here at night."

"You are so right, my little co-conspirator." The two of them giggled. "The plant vault isn't our problem anyway."

The key turned in the lock. The latch flapped open.

"Sweetie, try not to let Oulette get to you," Smalley soothed.

"I get so mad at him, bringing up what happened in France. It wasn't our fault. Oh, my you smell so nice tonight...." Their voices and footsteps echoed down the hallway.

"Come on, Cyd. Let's go."

Jane grabbed my arm. We ran down the hall, away from the lab, and out of the building. I was still panting when we got outside and the night air felt cold on my sweat-drenched hair. I never pedalled so hard in my life.

****

"Where do you think they keep those amphibians?" I called into the wind. It was the next day. We were riding our bikes and Jane was way ahead of me. "Jane!"

"Did you hear how she called him sweetie?" Jane yelled back as she slowed down. "Didn't that make you sick?"

"What do you think they'll do with all those frogs in the lab?" The sun glared in my eyes.

"Keep 'em I guess." Jane balanced on one pedal.

"I mean, during the day, when the other scientists are there. They can't keep them in that lab, so where do you think they'll hide them?"

"Yeah, that's a lot of frogs. How about on the roof? You know, the greenhouse. It takes up the entire floor. Mom said the gardener was off for the summer and the greenhouse was going to pot. The scientists wouldn't leave their plants there anymore." With that, she rode off.

"You're brilliant!" I yelled and pedaled hard to catch up with her.

Back home I checked the blog. "There's a comment on our latest blog entry. It's from Dakota again." I clicked it open.

122

***

Response to blog entry: <u>Itchy much? What's the buzz on all those mosquitoes?</u>

Look beyond the itch

It's not who's biting you

Who's not getting bit?

Ciao for now, Dakota.

***

"What is she talking about – 'Who's not getting bit?' We're all getting bit. Oh, she's had one too many latte and pain au chocolat."

That's Jane being not so impressed with Dakota's response. But I knew there was a clue in there somewhere.

"Let's do a search on frog experiments."

Jane gave me the if-looks-could-kill look.

"I know we agreed not to look up animal

123

experimentation." Jane had used Internet research about unnecessary experiments on animals in her argument against frog dissection. There was a lot of research being done on frogs that you didn't want to know about. "But we need to jump start our brains to get an idea of what their experiment is about. We've got nothing right now."

Jane nodded.

I started with a search on frog secretions. "Jane, look at this. There are tons of really cool experiments." She sauntered over. I continued going through the links.

"They use frog secretions for research into a treatment for diabetes, and immune diseases." I clicked on a new link. "This one talks about how amphibian skin is used by tribal peoples in the Amazon jungle because it has healing properties." There was a picture of an Amazonian Aboriginal person pressing a frog to his wound. "Well, who knew any of this?"

"I did, Cyd. It was all in my paper on why I wasn't going to dissect that frog. Frogs are like a walking pharmacy. Their skin is delicate because it needs to absorb water. They get infections really easily and bacteria can live on their skin. But, their skin is full of chemicals that keep them healthy. And some of that can be used for human diseases. That was in the section where I wrote about preserving animals to keep the bio-diversity..." Jane leaned over my shoulder.

"Yeah, blah, blah, bio-diversity, you sound like our parents. Next you'll have us doing a mystery, or should I say science project: Call of the Wild, the Exciting World of Bio-Diversity...."

"Hold on," Jane shouldered me out of the way and grabbed the laptop. She scrolled down the links like a maniac.

"This is it." She clicked on one.

Now I was peering over her shoulder. The headline looked like we wrote it.

"'Smelly Frog Skin – the next bug repellent'?" It was on a science news site. "It says that the frogs secrete 'anti-insect chemicals' from their skin."

I could use that, I thought scratching a mosquito bite.

"It says frog juice eventually could be used as bug juice." She swung around to face me. "The green liquid in the flask Smalley carried. That was frog juice to make bug juice." As if on cue, a swarm of mosquitoes landed on our bedroom screen window.

"That's what they're doing with the frogs. Extracting frog juice to make bug juice." She said it like a rhyme.

"And they probably came to our city because we have so many mosquitoes. That's it, Jane."

****

Feeling pretty good about ourselves for cracking the mystery, the next morning we convinced Mom to take us to the lab. We needed to do a forensic on the crime scene, er lab, from last night. We needed hard evidence.

"I'm so glad you girls are finally taking an interest in science. But really, I don't have anything exciting to do, just plant some seedlings, water some plants, monitor their growth, and make some notes." We were in her office. Mom's voice trailed as she turned her back to us and pulled stuff out of her briefcase.

"That's okay. Jane and I will hang out in the tropical greenhouse. You know how much we like those huge rubber tree plants."

"Okay, but not too long and then we'll go for ice cream." That's another thing we convinced Mom to do. She felt guilty working so much. But her working meant more time for us to solve the mystery, and it gave us a chance to hang out in the building.

Jane and I ditched Mom and headed for the lab. I scanned the lab and whispered. "Boy, it's a different place in the daylight when the Cheese Pie Man and Smalley aren't cooking up frog juice with Omelette."

"No sign of what went on the other night. No frogs, no croaking, no frog nappers. All the beakers are clean," observed Jane.

I glanced back over at Mom; she had her mind in her laptop. We wouldn't have to worry about her for a while. To make sure we were alone, we checked out the other labs down the hallway.

"Our mission today," I started, Jane grabbed her notebook she had her pencil ready, "is to get some evidence – like, a jug of frog/bug juice – and answer the last few questions we have ..."

Jane stopped writing and interrupted me, "And find out what happened to the frogs we saw yesterday."

Right, the frogs. Off to the rooftop greenhouse.

"We still don't know why it's such a secret if the research is on the Internet."

"Maybe they want to be the first to figure out a way to bottle it up and sell it. That's what they meant by riches. The jail part, hmmm?"

"We'll, maybe the jail part is because they are doing it in secret and probably didn't get the right approvals from the government or something."

We took the ancient service elevator. It was stuffy and smelled like mothballs. It had accordion style doors that we opened and closed ourselves, like in olden-days movies set in London. Usually, we pretended that we were in some great old castle in a gothic novel. But not today. We were on a mission.

The elevator went to the top floor of the building and then we climbed a stairway to the greenhouse. I listened as we hiked the steep stairs to the roof. Sun

129

shone through the stairwell from the greenhouse windows. The air was thick with humidity so the plants would think they were still on some tropical island instead of in the boring city. The door was propped open. We smelled that our hunch was right before we saw it. The stench grew stronger with each step and it reminded me of the snake exhibit at the zoo, slimy and oily. Finally, at the top of the stairs we walked through the door.

I couldn't believe my eyes. Frogs everywhere. Massive frogs! Enormous amphibians! I rubbed my eyes, mostly because the smell was making them sting, but also because I thought I was seeing things. I turned to look at Jane. She stood there with her backpack clutched to her chest.

Most of the frogs were the size of an oven. Some were the size of those small electric cars. Giant slimy green frog bodies squatted on the floor and on the plants. There were frogs everywhere. It was like *Planet of the Frogs* gone wild. Crushed tropical plants peeked out from under the frogs. Even the sides of the greenhouse seemed strained, since the frogs were stacked on top of each other. The water misters went off. Water trickled over the frogs and I swear they sighed with joy. My gut wrenched like a wet bathing suit wrung out. It was my worst nightmare come true. I should never have squished Jane's frog. Maybe it was their turn to step on me. My stomach flipped over. What was going on here?

The frogs croaked. *Loud* croaks, like car horns. I put my hands over my ears, then took one hand off and plugged my nose. I couldn't decide which was worse, the smell or the noise.

Jane talked but no words came out. Her mouth hung open like a flap on a mailbox. Frogs sprawled everywhere. They stopped trying to move. They

131

looked sad. "This is cruel," Jane shouted. "We have to do something."

My eyes watered from the smell. I thought I saw a frog making a move for me. "I don't know what to do, but let's get out of here," I said, holding my nose. "This is too weird."

A voice cut through the croaking.

"Looks good, Tallbot. Smelly, but good."

The voice froze my feet to the slimy goo covering the floor. Omelette spoke to the Cheese Pie Man. We crouched beside a frog. My knees pressed against its oily skin. I could feel its cold-blooded breath on my arm. I held my arm closer to my body.

"If your concoction of the growth hormone worked this well after three days, I think you can tweak it to get them to the size we want. Dial it down a few notches, I don't want people to think something fishy is going on, or should I say *froggy*." He let out a snort

132

and slapped Dr. Tallbot on the back. "Now get rid of these, and start working on the next batch.I am ready to buy the formula from you now."

"No!" Jane shrieked. She jumped up.

I grabbed her arm but it was too late, Omelette and the Cheese Pie Man stared at her. The look of shock on their faces turned to anger. Sometimes it was tough having a twin who was an animal lover.

"What are you kids doing in here?" cried Mr. Oulette. He swerved to face Tallbot. "I thought this floor was off-limits," he spat.

The Cheese Pie Man took one look at me and screamed. He ran right for me. There was no way around so he started to climb over the animals. He slipped on the back of a frog and his body made a slapping sound when he landed. He struggled to get up, managed to stand, and tried to run toward me again. Anger darted from his eyes. He groaned as he strained to run and keep his balance, then fell face first on the next frog. A vial of formula sprung from his pizza dough hand and soared through air. It landed with a soft thump on the back of the frog we stood behind.

"Ribbit," croaked the frog.

Jane must have taken that as some kind of sign from the spirit of her dead frog because she scooped up the vial, grabbed me and ran.

I peered back when we were a few steps down the stairs. The Cheese Pie Man was on his feet. He slipped and climbed over the frogs as he scrambled his way across the greenhouse.

"Stop them. They've got the formula," he bellowed.

From then on, I didn't look back. We ran down the rest of the steep steps, the smell, and noise faded with each step. I yanked open the doors to the elevator.

134

The formula glowed in Jane's fist. She held it so tightly that I was afraid it would break and she would become the incredible growing, bug repellent twin. I slammed the doors shut behind us and pressed the button for the floor of Mom's lab. I swallowed a big gulp of air. The sound of my heartbeat echoed in my ears like a chorus of steel drums. The elevator creaked and groaned into action.

Dr. Tallbot must have taken the stairs because he was waiting for us when the elevator doors opened. Maybe he rolled down the stairs. How else could such a large man beat an elevator?

"Hello, girls." He smiled and pushed back a lock of his sweat-drenched hair from his face. He gasped for breath and his body blocked the elevator door. Trapped inside the elevator, Jane slipped the vial into her pocket. Her hands shook.

"You go right, I'll go left," I whispered to Jane.

135

Tallbot tried to grab for both of us. He caught the back of my T-shirt but I twisted free. We slipped through his sausage-sized fingers and ran down the hall. "Mom!" I called.

"*There* you girls are. Perfect timing. I'm ready to go."

"No, wait, we have to tell you something." I tried to catch my breath. I could hear the heavy steps of the Cheese Pie Man as he clomped up behind us. What would he do with our mom there? Jane and I stood close by her side.

"Why, Bert. What brings you down to the lab on this beautiful Saturday afternoon? All of a sudden, my girls are interested in science. Isn't that nice?"

"Lovely," he puffed. He yanked a handkerchief from his shirt pocket and wiped the sweat from his brow. "I ran into them in the greenhouse."

The Cheese Pie Man put his hand on my shoulder

and squeezed. I squirmed out of his grip. Would he tell Mom about the vial? Our eyes locked like a vice-like grip. If he mentioned the vial, I'd spill my guts about the frogs.

"They probably didn't know, but the top floor greenhouse is off-limits from now on. I have my experiments up there," said Tallbot.

"Sorry, Bert. I didn't know that. Next time, I'll keep the girls with me," Mom replied. "Or put them to work and they'll have to help me with my experiments." He and Mom laughed. But his was a fake laugh. The one grown-ups do when things really aren't funny.

Tallbot looked me dead in the eye and whispered under his breath, "Maybe next time they will be the subjects of the experiment." He squeezed my shoulder again and this time his grip stuck. It felt like it would leave fingerprints on my shoulder. My spine felt like a Popsicle.

Chapter Eleven
Dead Frog in a Drawer

Blog Entry: <u>Why giant frogs?</u>

Green slimy frog body

Stretched like an elastic band

Why would you want to?

***

We'd see what Dakota had to say about *that* Haiku. I pulled the digital camera cable from the computer and shoved it in a drawer. With notebooks in hand we headed to the museum to search for answers to what we saw yesterday.

"Open This Drawer," Jane read. "Ahh ..." she shouted as she opened it. A frog jiggled around in formaldehyde. "That's gross," said Jane.

I slammed the drawer shut. "Do you think a real detective would get grossed out by a little dead frog in a drawer? The ones in the greenhouse were as big as our oven. Besides, we shouldn't be wasting our time here. Now that the Cheese Pie Man knows that we know he's creating giant frogs, and that we have the vial of formula, he'll be after us," I ran out of breath. Why was I the freak-out twin now? Maybe it was Tallbot's snakebite grip from yesterday afternoon, where my shoulder still hurt.

"Cyd, relax, we need to do a little research before we go back to Mom or the police. If we could find out more about frogs, we might be able to figure out why they need the frogs so big? Maybe there is a scientific angle."

"Bigger frog means more frog secretions and more bug juice. First they create giant frogs; then they skim the frog juice off of the slimy skin. They'll have giant crates of bug juice. We don't need to do any more research. No frog grows to be as big as the ones Smalley and the Cheese Pie Man cooked up. Plus, Omelette – the French restaurant angle. There's nothing scientific about that."

Jane pretty much ignored me and wandered around the other exhibits jotting down a note or two here and there, acting all detective like. "Why is Omelette involved? That's one thing we don't know."

There were swarms of kids with their parents. They touched the displays of animal skins, and peered in other drawers that contained equally gross exhibits of animals in formaldehyde.

"Why did Omelette say they should get rid of those frogs? Wouldn't they keep these frogs and scrape the slime off their skin or something?" I opened the drawer again; the sign said it was a Striped Chorus Frog. I zoned in on the frog. It looked like the late Frogzilla. They were common throughout the prairies and in the foothills. Funny, it didn't say they grew to be immense amphibians of the Cheese Pie Man variety.

I went to find Jane. She peered into the insect display. There were some neat insects, like the ones that looked like wood for perfect camouflage.

"Hey, wait a minute." I grabbed Jane by the arm and spun her around to face me. "I've got it. Let's ditch this place and head to the library." She looked confused but she was knee-deep in toddlers and took my lead to leave.

Read a Book! Unleash Your Imagination read the sign in the library. Unleash it? Who were they kidding?

I had been trying to get my imagination under control since yesterday. Last night I dreamt I was a princess and a giant frog was trying to kiss me. I couldn't do it. Imagine how big the prince would be. I ran and ran and the giant lumbering frog hopped after me and croaked. I couldn't wait to wake up.

"Come on, the Natural Science section is over here." I was first in our class to learn the Dewey Decimal system, and Jane the Internet. I searched through the stacks of books.

"Cyd, what are you looking for? Let me in on it."

"Camouflage. Don't you get it? That's the key." I ran my fingers over the spines of the books. "Formula, how to create a formula, that's what I need. We hide the real formula in the house. Then we create a fake formula, and carry it around with us. When the Cheese Pie Man catches up to us – and he will," I stopped searching and glared at Jane for effect, "He gets the fake formula. We still have the real one and can give it to the police for their investigation, and then the court case." I was on a roll now. "Just need a book on how to create a fake formula ..."

"Why don't we use juice?" suggested Jane.

"*Juice.* Of course." I hit my forehead with the palm of my hand. "Now that's the kind of thinking we need on this case." I gave Jane a quick hug. We headed for the door.

"Look, it's Frogzilla, I mean the Striped Chorus Frog." Jane had got sidetracked by a book that was open on the table. The Striped Chorus Frog was a regular sized frog, like they're supposed to be, like Frogzilla was. She flipped the book over to see the title, *The Wonderful World of Amphibians*, then leafed through it.

I was halfway to the door.

"Look, Cyd, frogs of every size and color. Not giant, fridge size, Cheese Pie Man frogs. Listen to this," she read, "... the croak of the Chorus Frog is a drawn out rasping, like the sound of a thumbnail being drawn slowly over the teeth of a comb. That's exactly how Frogzilla sounded." Jane slammed the book shut. "Now that we know what they're up to we have to find a way to stop them. They don't need frogs that big to make bug spray."

"Unless he's entering those frogs into a giant frog-jumping contest, he's up to no good. At least we can discount the virus-in-the-water-supply theory."

"Be serious, Cyd. You remember what the newspaper article said about the experiments being harmful to both the animal and human population. What are they going to do with these giant frogs that could harm people? What if the bug spray doesn't work? Plus, they work in Mom's lab. What if she gets in their way and, and ...."

"Okay, okay, I get it." I didn't want her to finish her sentence. What if Mom did get in the way? Nancy Drew always got hit, half-drowned or thrown out of a car in her mysteries, but I wasn't up for that. Mosquito-ravaged skin was my limit. We needed that fake formula.

"We've got to try to tell Mom again," said Jane.

"No. You know how mad she was. She thought we were lying. That didn't feel good. She's a scientist. We need some hard evidence to convince her. In the meantime, we also need to keep the real formula out of the hands of the Cheese Pie Man."

"How much more evidence do we need? We saw them with our own eyes, smelled them with our own noses, heard them with our own ears ..."

"Okay, I get it, you don't have to go through all

five senses," I said.

Jane said stubbornly, "Once we explain to her what these people are like she'll stay away from them. She'll tell her boss, maybe she'll go to the police. We've got to try to tell her again."

I looked at the frogs on the cover of the book, and then I thought about the frogs they were experimenting on in the lab. We knew they were making bug juice, but something was terribly wrong. "Just a few more days. If we can get some more evidence, we'll convince her. Let's start on that formula."

Jane breathed a little easier.

Chapter Twelve
Rewarding Career in Law Enforcement

Response to Blog Entry: <u>Why Giant Frogs?</u>

Why not giant frogs?

Butter wrapped around quails

Garlic laced snails

Signed: **It's Dakota's dinnertime!**

****

"Mom?"

"Yes, dear." She put down a copy of *Genetics R Us* magazine and sat up, making room for me on the couch. Jane was right behind me. "What is it?"

"Oh, nothing." I turned to leave. Jane pushed me back. Why did I always have to be the brave one? I hopped up and sat down beside Mom.

"Have you noticed anything funny about Bert Tallbot and Rita Smalley?"

"Oh, not this again." She picked up her magazine and started leafing through the pages. I'd lost her.

"Mom, you said we could tell you anything. We noticed something funny at the lab, in the greenhouse …." This got her attention.

"Funny? What do you mean by funny?"

"Well, like for instance, he said his experiments are in the greenhouse. Why would he need the whole greenhouse for his experiments?"

"He and Rita are making a presentation about their work to the rest of the lab next week. I guess I'll find out what I need to know then." She stuck her nose back in the magazine.

This was getting me nowhere. "Did you happen to notice that he smells like an amphibian?" I like to take the direct approach. Jane's bony fingers dug into my ribs.

"Cynthia, that's a horrible thing to say ...."

"Mom, we know that Rita Smalley and Bert Tallbot are experimenting on frogs. Making them grow to enormous sizes." I stretched my hands out to show her how big the frogs were. But I don't have my dad's long arms so I couldn't get my hands wide enough. Mom sighed. She wasn't mad this time, just exasperated.

"Some kind of formula, maybe a growth hormone, something to do with all the mosquitoes," Jane said, sitting down and squeezing me closer to Mom on the couch.

"Is that why you're so interested in coming to the lab?" She closed her magazine and slapped it down on the coffee table. She put on her scientist face. Here comes the lecture.

"Look, so what if they're doing experiments on frogs. Scientists have experimented with growth hormones for years. There have been many advances for the farming industry and other areas as well, even medical science benefits for children. It's not something to be scared of. It's not against the law. Sure there's a lot of mosquitoes this year, but that's Mother Nature. Bert and Rita came to the university with the highest recommendations. It wouldn't do you any harm to spend some time with them, talk to them about their research and university science programs."

"But Oulette's in on the plot as well and there's a formula in a test tube ..." I blurted out.

"Okay, that's enough: Mr. Oulette is a trusted business man. Who cares if he's a friend of Bert and Rita's?"

150

Who cares indeed? That sounded like one of those rhetorical questions; questions that didn't need an answer. I wasn't about to answer it.

"I know you girls are old enough to stay on your own while I'm at work, but I think you need more structured activities. I'm glad that you read a lot and want to be writers. I liked Nancy Drew as much as the next person when I was little, but enough already with the Nancy Drew plots and the Nancy Drew Home Page. There's a nice sleep-over camp at the zoo..." she leafed through the mail on the coffee table "...let me find the pamphlet here." She found it and went to the kitchen to make the phone call. "And I want a field trip report when you're back. Two pages each. That should keep you busy. You can do it like it's a, what do you call it, a 'zine, or something?" Her voice trailed.

"Blog. Blog!" I cried after her.

Jane scowled at me. "Way to go, Cyd. Now what

do we do?"

"*Me* ... what are you talking about? Okay, okay. I don't know. How about plan B?"

****

For a rewarding career in law enforcement, contact your local police station. I stopped and read the sign on the entrance door. "Why do we have to go to the police? Mom didn't believe us. They won't either. We can solve this on our own."

"Nancy Drew always went to the police when she needed them. They worked together."

"Only in the old-school version of the books would Chief McGuiness work with Nancy. In the newer series, Chief McGuiness is her enemy. Nancy solves all the mysteries before he does, and that threatens him."

"That's great, Cyd, but Nancy Drew never had the likes of the Cheese Pie Man and his giant amphibians to deal with. Plus, we're not getting any help on the clues we're posting on our blog. What was Dakota's latest answer: snails and quails? Throw in some puppy dog tails and she's got a nursery rhyme."

I thought about this for a moment, decided that Jane's sarcasm gene had just kicked in, and then pushed open the door.

"Well, hello, girls," boomed the voice of a police officer. "What can I do for you today? Lost puppy, stolen bike? You know, too many children leave their bikes lying on the front lawn."

"No sir," I interrupted. "We're here about something else."

"Something far more serious, crimes against the animal kingdom," Jane said. "We'd like to speak to Deputy Dan and his police dog, Dawber."

"Who?"

"He came to our first grade class to talk about

how police officers are your friends. You know, Deputy Dan and his..."

"Oh, right. He's on assignment, sniffing out some criminal activity. Will I do? I'm a detective. I'm a good friend of Deputy Dan's, and Dawber really likes me."

"There's this scientist, the Cheese Pie Man..."

Jane poked me in the ribs with her bony fingers.

"Er, I mean Dr. Tallbot," I said.

The detective took out his notepad and jotted notes.

"He's creating giant frogs."

He lifted his pen from the pad and looked at us.

"It's true," piped up Jane. "We saw them at our mother's lab, in the greenhouse. We have the formula, only we're going to make a fake..."

He slapped his notebook shut. It sounded like a laugh.

"Look girls, even if this is true, and I'm not saying it's not, but even if it is, it's not a crime for scientists to create things. They do it all the time. Why, look at those giant tomatoes. Great invention. And those cows that give more milk. Kids like milk right? Now why don't you take a ride in the park?"

"But all the mosquitoes?" Jane made one last attempt.

"Pesky little devils, I'll agree with you on that one." He opened his desk drawer, rummaged around and pulled out two junior Deputy Dan badges, like the ones we got in grade one.

"Doesn't he know we're too old for these?" I said as the detective closed the door behind us.

"Yeah, and besides, I still have mine."

"Nancy Drew gets way more respect. Well,

there's only one thing left to do." I jumped on my bike and pedalled. "It's called *The Mystery of How to Make a Fake Formula That will Trap the Evil Scientists and Stop them from Creating More Giant Frogs* – from the Cyd files," I shouted back into the wind. Okay, little long for a title, but if Nancy Drew could solve a mystery by herself then so could we.

"It's the Cyd and Jane files. Wait up," Jane yelled.

Chapter Thirteen
Safari Sleepover

Blog Entry: <u>Donuts R Us</u>

Police don't care much

Donuts, round, full of sugar

We're on our own now.

****

"I thought Mom would be all over our discovery. She's all about DNA. Hand me the fruit punch." We were in the kitchen. I concocted the fake formula and Jane packed up our lunch for the Safari sleepover.

"But it's not a DNA experiment. They would have to manipulate the DNA by genetically modifying the egg to create giant frogs. They are using a formula that we think is a growth hormone. For a growth hormone to work they would repeatedly inject it into the animal. That's what it looks like they're doing."

I nearly dropped the test tube. "So you've actually been listening to Mom and Dad's dinner time 'science topic' of the day? We agreed that we'd just humor them with this science stuff. Once we show an interest, that's all we'll hear about. Then they'll be taking us to science conferences, hiring us as junior lab assistants. It won't stop there. Do you want a lifetime subscription to *How to Make a Scientist Out of Your Kid*? It's embarrassing enough that our experiments always win the science contests just because we know more about science than most kids."

"I get it, Cyd. That's enough, already."

I caught my breath and looked down at the fake formula I was trying to create. "Well, it's just that all that science stuff will take us away from our writing."

"*Your* writing. I'm just trying to figure out what's up with the frogs. Besides do you know what the inside of the large mammal house smells like?" Jane asked.

"Sure, I know. How could I not know? I've been there just as often as you have, which is every time Mom or Dad has a free moment. We've been there so often that I don't even need the map they give you at the front gate. You'd think there was nothing else to do in this city," I snapped.

"Well, whose idea was the Safari sleepover at the zoo?"

"Are you blaming me for that? What do you mean, 'Whose idea was it?' It was your idea to tell Mom and it backfired. She didn't believe us. The police didn't take us seriously. Now we'll be stuck with a bunch of goofy kids at the zoo," I said.

Jane handed me a bag full of graham wafers with peanut butter and jam. "Yeah, but at least I didn't blurt it out like you did. If you'd stuck to my plan we'd be solving this mystery instead of going to camp," she mumbled, as she turned away and stuffed the lunch in her backpack.

I'd gone too far. "Okay, I'm sorry."

We always had peanut butter and jam graham wafers when we were little, but Mom hadn't made them for us since grade one. That's when they tried to put us in separate classes. Jane said we couldn't be apart because we were twins and had the same blood– and besides, she had all the graham wafers. Since then we've always been in the same class.

The graham wafers squished around in the bag. "Look, it might be fun."

"No, Cyd, you're right. This is baby stuff. We

won't find out anything wasting our time at the zoo."

"Well, don't they have an amphibian exhibit? Maybe we can sneak away and do some research."

"Let's worry about that tonight. You finish the fake formula and we'll find a place to hide the real one," Jane said.

I went back to the mess I'd created on the counter. "Now a little bit of apple juice, a touch of maple syrup, a drop of green food coloring, and we're done. One more stir. There." I held the jar up against the vial of real formula. "Looks exactly the same. Great."

An almost empty bottle of vanilla was on the counter. It was the right size for the formula in the vial. I rinsed the bottle out and poured the formula in. I was careful to get all of it. Then I rinsed the vial and filled it with the fake formula.

Jane packed her mystery novel and her notepad. I slid the fake formula across the counter. "Pack this in the side pocket of your backpack. If we run into the Cheese Pie Man anywhere, we'll know the real formula is safe." I put the vanilla bottle back in the cupboard with the spices. No fear of Mom making cookies; Jane and I did most of the baking. It was like science, we told our parents. lots of measuring, only with chocolate chips.

Jane flipped open the laptop on the kitchen table.

"Are you checking our blog? Let's look at it before we head out."

"Not yet. I want to re-read that website about the bug spray research. Maybe it will lead us to a clue," explained Jane.

She pointed at the screen. "It's research being done in Australia. Here we go, Cyd, look at this. It says one of the problems with selling the bug juice made from frog juice is that it smells really bad."

I shoved Jane away from the screen. "'Some frog secretions can smell like rotting meat.' Yuck. 'Others smell like nuts and thyme leaves.' Well, that's all right."

Jane edged me aside. "Turns out that frogs have more than one type of slime. The challenge is to isolate the exact frog slime that bugs don't like. I haven't noticed any smell coming off of the formula, have you?"

"Nah." I was bored with this already. I closed down the site. This wasn't leading anywhere.

"There's that herb smell that Rita has. You remember how the Cheese Pie Man kept telling her how sweet she smelled."

"I think she smells like cat food."

"Let's check our blog. Maybe Dakota has left another clue."

The blog opened on a digital of Frogzilla with

R.I.P. written under it. I shuddered. Jane must have changed our dashboard. The cute digital of Jane and me was gone.

****

Response to Blog Entry: <u>Donuts R Us</u>

Hey girls, I'm bored with this Haiku challenge. You win as always, Cyd. Forget about donuts. Try a chocolate croissant! There's got to be something interesting to blog about. France is fabulous. The food is unusual, very experimental.

Ciao till later, Dakota.

****

"What? She doesn't get it. Those weren't clues she was giving us, just Haikus. Now we're no further ahead."

"No, they were clues. That's what gets me."

"Well, you got *us*, Cyd—stuck on a Safari sleepover. We need to go."

We were on our own with this mystery and, if I didn't play my cards right, I'd be on *my* own.

****

The zoo was different at night. Quieter. It was empty except for twelve kids our age and the Safari sleepover camp leader. He spotted us and headed our way.

"I'm Todd," he stuck out his hand, "leader of this here camp, little dogies." He tried to do a western drawl and failed spectacularly. Tall, skinny Todd was dressed in khakis, as if he was bushwhacking through the Amazon jungle, not leading a Safari sleepover at the zoo. A water jug was slung across this chest like a rifle.

"Cyd," I said as I shook the teenager's sweaty hand. "And my twin, Jane."

"Yes, I know. I recognized your names from the registration list." He showed off his clipboard. "I'm a

165

high school student, working here for the summer. I took a class at mini-university from your mom. Both your parents are esteemed."

If "esteemed" meant full of hot air, this guy was full of it. Todd was like the science-nerd older brother we didn't have but our parents would love to adopt. I wondered if he was an orphan.

"So, what are you supposed to do if one of those mammals gets out of their cage? Call Smoky the Bear?" I shot some air out of his esteem as I wiped the sweat on my hand off on my shorts.

He fake-laughed. "I printed some research off the 'net for you girls. I thought you'd be interested in the latest findings on animals in captivity. Maybe I can meet your mom, er, both your parents sometime?"

The sun set over the trees the giraffes were eating. I ignored Todd since he was as annoying as the cloud of mosquitoes that landed on us. Jane chatted

166

him up. Seems they both had an interest in small talk.

The only animals in captivity I was interested in were the ones the Cheese Pie Man was experimenting on, and I wasn't about to find out anything wasting my time at the zoo. We swatted mosquitoes all the way to the Large Mammal house. Inside, snorts and snuffles of the wild animals echoed in the room. That's what they were, after all, wild animals, and here we were about to sleep on a cot beside them.

Elephants, rhinoceri, hippopotami, and giraffes. The smell was worse than I imagined. I had a flashback to the greenhouse. Could I sleep and hold my nose at the same time? The Large Mammal house was much bigger than a normal house. It was gigantic, tall enough for the giraffes and wide enough for the elephants. There were huge doors so that the animals could go outside to the compounds during the day and then come in at night.

I stared into the hippo enclosure. "This is really creepy, Jane." I expected to see giant amphibians everywhere. "They may be that big by now," I pointed to the hippo. He flashed me his giant yellow teeth. What was the Cheese Pie Man up to that he was growing frogs that big?

"Let's set our stuff up outside," I suggested. "That way we'll be safer. There's no telling what these animals do at night. Besides, we'll need to sneak out to go to the amphibian exhibit."

"But what if we get caught and they send us home and Mom can't get a refund?"

That's the Jane I knew. It was good to have her back to her old, worrywart self.

"They'll never notice."

"Children, we're about to start our program for the evening." Todd clapped his hands to get our attention. "I know this is a Safari sleepover," he emphasized the word *safari*, "but we're lucky to have a visiting professor who is an expert on amphibians."

"Amphibians," I whispered to Jane.

"May I present to you—Dr. Bert Tallbot!" Todd announced with a flourish.

We swung around toward the door. The Cheese Pie Man waddled in. Todd scooted over and half-bowed as he tried to shake Tallbot's hand. Tallbot brushed him away like he was hornet at a picnic.

"Isn't he bigger than the last time we saw him?" His feet strained the laces of his shoes.

"No, you're crazy," Jane laughed. Then her laugh turned into a gasp. "The formula is safe, right?" Jane grabbed my hand and squeezed. I felt her tremble.

"Yeah, the formula is safe. Remember the vanilla...? It's all right; he won't dare bother us with all these people around."

Jane took a deep breath and seemed to calm

down. "Besides, if he doesn't watch out, the hippos will adopt him." Jane swallowed a nervous giggle behind her hand.

Todd said pompously, "Gather round, children. Dr. Tallbot will talk to us and then you can ask him questions. Maybe he can tell us why there aren't many frogs this year in the river valley."

We joined the group and sat at the back. We didn't want him to spot us. Without Mom around, we didn't dare risk it. Even with the formula hidden, there was no telling what Tallbot would do if he found out we were there.

The Cheese Pie Man mumbled on about the different types of amphibians found in our city. Funny though, he didn't mention the mutant oversized ones he grew in his lab.

"Maybe he's growing them big because he wants some company," Jane whispered and promptly squealed with laughter. She'd never learned the art of laughing quietly. An attack of the giggles would be next.

I put my hand over Jane's mouth. She lost her balance and fell over on her back. She still had her backpack on. There was a sound like chalk scratching on a black board. *It was the vial.* Jane must have left the side pocket unzipped. It fell out and landed at her feet on the concrete floor. She jumped up and almost stepped on it. I got up on my knees and tried to pull her out of sight.

The Cheese Pie Man stopped talking. All eyes were on us. The Cheese Pie Man glared at us so hard I thought my head would explode. Then a smile spread over his face. He went back to his lecture and the kids stopped staring. "I hope he isn't on the Safari sleepover," I whispered as I scooped up the vial and hid it in my backpack.

Chapter Fourteen
Snakes R Us

The Cheese Pie Man split right after his lecture. "Where do you think he's gone?" Jane asked. She looked over her shoulder and up in the trees as if the Cheese Pie Man would swing down like a gorilla. "It was weird how the he left like that. I thought for sure he would try to get the vial."

Todd gave us two choices after the lecture: watch a movie on the elephants of Africa, or explore the Amphibian and Reptile House at feeding time. Not a tough decision for Jane and me. It turned out that we were the only ones heading to the Amphibian and Reptile House. Todd told us to go on without him, and that he'd join us when the movie was rolling. The animal feeder would meet us at the front door.

I heard a branch crack and I swung around. Nothing there. A breeze ruffled my jacket. I pulled it tighter around me, slung my backpack off my shoulder and hugged it to my chest. The formula was fake, but I didn't want the next blog entry title to read: *Attack of the Cheese Pie Man.* I couldn't imagine what picture I would upload to go along with that entry.

"That's strange. Why is this door at the back of the building open? *Private – Animal Feeders Only,*" Jane read.

The door creaked when I pushed it open for a peek inside. "Looks like the feeder isn't here yet."

I opened the door all the way and walked in.

"I bet this is where they keep all the mice."

"Don't try to gross me out, Cyd. Everyone knows that snakes eat mice. But last time I was here they told me that they never feed them *live* mice, only dead ones."

The door clicked shut behind us. We swung around.

The python hissed.

So did Tallbot, holding it. "I want the vial," he spat.

The python's head was in one hand, its body wrapped around his shoulders, and its tail in his other hand.

My blood froze in my veins. This must be what it felt like to be a reptile. I couldn't move.

Jane grabbed my arm and hid behind me. The snake's tongue darted in and out of its mouth. Tallbot's smile matched the snake's. Jane squeezed my arm

174

tighter and sucked in her breath.

Tallbot sneered, "Your mother told me you'd be here tonight. She bragged about your new-found interest in science."

"Someone will be here soon to feed the animals." My words sounded like a frightened squeak.

"He won't be bothering us." Tallbot motioned to the side. A man's feet stuck out from under the table.

I walked sideways out of the animal feeder room toward the exhibit hall. I pushed Jane through the door. We were in the exhibit hall now.

The Cheese Pie Man followed. "It's no use. There's no way out and no one here to rescue you. I locked the main door." He lurched closer and the snake writhed in his hand. He smirked. "I knew you were too snoopy to pass up an open door. Thought you'd find a mystery behind it, didn't you? It doesn't pay to pry

175

into other people's business, now does it? *I want the vial.*"

I backed into the glass exhibits. Jane was in front of me. I inched my way along, looking for an escape route. I squeezed my backpack harder against my chest. Maybe I should give him the vial; the formula was a fake, after all. My legs shook. I walked backward. He followed. The snake swayed like in the movies with the snake charmer.

"Would you like to hold my friend? He can squeeze the life out of you. He can swallow a rabbit whole." He threw his head back and laughed. The laugh bounced off the glass exhibits of the other snakes, lizards, and frogs.

We were close to the front entrance door in the main gallery. Jane's nails bit into my arm. The glass exhibit, right behind, which normally housed the python, was empty. The window to the exhibit behind us was open. There was nowhere to go.

"Maybe you need some convincing." He darted forward, grabbed Jane from me, and then pulled her toward him. She let out a yelp I've only heard when she has nightmares. The snake's tongue darted out and brushed Jane's cheek.

"Give it to him," she cried.

Jane meant the vial. But he had my twin. I gave it to him all right! I dropped the backpack and ran at him. I leapt on him and hit him with all my might. I punched soft Cheese Pie Man flesh and slimy snake body. My eyes blinded with fear. The snake slithered onto Jane's shoulder. It inched toward her neck. I pummelled him. My punches bounced off the Cheese Pie Man like he was an inflatable tire tube. Jane stood still but looked like she was going to explode. Pythons killed by suffocation.

"Had enough?" Tallbot prodded Jane.

177

"Give it to him!" Jane screamed—and then winked.

I slid off Tallbot and the snake. Storming back to where I dropped the backpack, I ripped open the side pocket and grabbed the vial. It was warm, and a little sticky. "All right Tallbot. Drop the twin." I laid the vial on a table outside of his reach. He eased his grasp on Jane and she darted back to me.

The vial disappeared into his doughy hand. He pulled out the cork and smelled it. The snake lolled around his shoulders. He tried to dip his pinkie finger in the vial. It wouldn't fit. Tallbot dripped a bit of the formula on his index finger and darted his tongue out to taste it.

Jane and I looked at each other. Cheese Pie Man wasn't dumb. In fact, he was an evil genius. It wouldn't take him long to figure out the formula was a fake.

"This is a kid's drink." Tallbot licked the top of his

mouth like peanut butter was stuck to it. "What's that sticky stuff?" He gave it another lick. "Maple syrup!" He looked madder than if we had taken the syrup right off his pancakes. "Where's the real formula?" Tallbot bellowed.

We had to get out of there. I heard a faint click. A key turned in the lock.

"There you two are. Sorry it took so long. I couldn't get the film loaded the right way," said Todd.

Grabbing Jane's hand, I shot her a glance that said, *be ready to make a run for it.*

"I guess the animal feeder let you in. Oh..." Todd stopped when he saw Tallbot and the python. The Cheese Pie Man pocketed the test tube. Todd glanced at us then looked back at Tallbot and the snake. Doubt flashed across his face.

"Why Dr. Tallbot ... I didn't expect to see you

179

here. You said you were just getting a breath of fresh air. Don't tell me you're a snake expert as well? Hey, thanks for showing these girls the python. I was tied up."

Tied up! Two more minutes and we'd have been tied tighter than a skate lace.

"Oh, yes, I have an interest in all living things. And I was on my way back to give you my security clearance forms." Tallbot pulled out some crinkled pages from his pocket and shoved them at Todd.

It was the voice he used with our mother. The marshmallows-in-hot-chocolate voice. With the snake still wrapped around his shoulders like a slimy scarf, the Cheese Pie Man didn't take his eyes off us.

"The girls and I were just having a nice chat about reptiles. I'll bring them back to the Mammal House when we're done."

"That would be generous of you, Dr. Tallbot.

180

I'll go back and supervise the others." Todd started reading the security forms as he turned to leave. "Wait, these pages are blank …" Todd turned back to face us. He would never believe what had happened before he arrived. Jane looked at me desperately. I had to think fast.

Just then, the snake retched. It sounded like Yin when she was warming up to hurl a hairball. It wriggled. Tallbot struggled to hold on to the wriggling snake. The python's mouth opened wide like it was on a hinge. So that's how they swallowed things whole. It retched again. Bile dripped from his mouth. We stood there stunned, grossed out, but mesmerised at the same time. It retched for the last time, and then the snake vomited up what looked like a small village of rodents. The mass of mice and bile fell to the floor with a plop.

I thought I'd lose every lunch I'd ever had, but

this was our chance to get out of there. Jane and I clamped eyes and bolted for the door. I grabbed my backpack and held it against my chest as I ran. Out of the corner of my eye, I saw the animal feeder come out of the back room. He rubbed his head. He'd be all right. And I'm sure Tallbot would slither his way out of this. Let Todd and his clipboard sort out Tallbot, the animal feeder, and the snake tonight.

We went back to the sleepover.

"This snake stuff is messy business," was all Jane said. She looked pale.

"Yeah, I can see the blog entry title now: *Twins stick Cheese Pie Man with a little syrup.*"

But Jane didn't find that funny. She didn't speak the rest of the time we were on the sleepover.

It would be days before Jane would be able to talk about what happened with the snake, and days before I would mention it.

I stuck close to her. We left the zoo as soon as the morning feeding was over.

What would Tallbot do now that he knew we still had the real formula?

Chapter Fifteen
Basted Ribs

By the time we got home, it was noon. I had my key ready but the door was unlocked. It wasn't like Mom to leave it that way. I inched the door open and looked around for Mom.

Dr. Tallbot stood in our front hallway.

When Jane saw him, she screamed. Then I saw him and screamed, too. Jane grabbed on to the back of my shirt and hid behind me.

"Hello girls," smiled Bert Tallbot. "So good to see you again."

"Where's our mother? What have you done with her?"

He pulled a meat cleaver from behind his back. He plucked the blade with his finger like he was strumming a guitar string. Blood stained the knife and remnants of flesh hung from it.

"She's basting in the kitchen." He grinned.

"AAA!" We screamed again.

"Girls, girls. What is all the commotion about? Pipe down," said Mom.

"Mom!" We ran and hugged her, something we hadn't done in a long time. It felt safe.

"You were only gone one night. What's all the fuss about?"

"But we thought ...."

"Oh, did I forget to mention that I invited Bert, Rita and Cam over for a barbecue this afternoon? They came early to help out. Dr. Tallbot was cutting the ribs and Mr. Oulette and I just finished basting them. Go wash up. You smell like eels."

Oulette popped his head out of the kitchen and pinched the sides of his nose. "Ewww, you need some of my sweet smelling herbs for your bath water. They only grow in my village, on my grandmother's land."

We dragged our bodies up the stairs, too tired to make it to Control Central. It had been a long night, what with the near-death experience of my twin and all. Now this. It was too much.

"What's going on? What does he want with us? How dare he come here?" With a sudden burst of energy, Jane paced back and forth in our room. I hoped there was a guarantee on that rug because she was causing it serious wear and tear. "What is he up to? I don't want to leave Mom alone with him." She plopped down on her bed.

"Calm down, Jane." I grabbed her by both

186

shoulders. I was going to shake her but then I saw the look in her eye and hugged her. "It'll be all right. He's freaking us out. We'll go downstairs and, in our best amateur girl detective composure, we'll sit through dinner. He won't get the best of us." I said the words, and then I tried hard to believe them. It wasn't fair, though. I don't remember one Nancy Drew book where she had to eat barbecued ribs with a known villain.

"I've got to blog about this. Maybe Dakota will clue into something we're missing:

Blog Entry: <u>Snakes R Us</u>

You are a snake too

Slither 'round my neck

I just can't prove it.

187

I wanted to download a cartoon snake from the computer's graphics program just to lighten things up. But Jane was in a hurry to get downstairs.

****

The kitchen smelled wonderful, like warm barbecue sauce. The Cheese Pie Man, and Omelette stirred a pot of sauce. Mom measured an ingredient like she was in her lab and handed it to Smalley. They drank wine and chatted, having a great old time.

Dinner was my chance to find out what was going on. Maybe my last chance, I thought, as Tallbot glared at me. He licked the spoon and put it back in for one more stir. Gross. A double dipper. I took my place at the table.

"I have never tasted such succulent ribs," Tallbot slurped the sauce off his fingers. "You must give me the recipe," he smiled at Oulette.

Yeah, and the Cheese Pie Man would cook up

a batch of giant cows in his lab. Tallbot sawed huge pieces of meat and put the biggest piece possible in his mouth at one time.

"I don't mind telling you the secret ingredient," said Oulette: "It's vanilla."

Vanilla! Jane and I looked at each other. Her eyes were the size of pancakes. I dropped a fork full of ribs onto my plate. Startled by the clang, the Cheese Pie Man looked up from his ribs, and then smirked. He was on to us.

"Did you use up *all* our vanilla?" I blurted out. All eyes were on me. My mom shot me the stink eye. I lowered my voice and tried to sound calm. "I might want to make cookies later."

"Cynthia, that's rude. Mr. Oulette can use anything in our house if he's making ribs this succulent." Mom shoved a large piece of meat into her mouth and chewed. A dribble of sauce shot out of the corner of her mouth and landed on her chin. She wiped it up with her finger and licked it. Was she turning into the Cheese Pie Man? Or even worse, would she turn into the incredible gigantic mommy?

"I always bring my own vanilla," Oulette assured me. "They make it in the village I grew up in. It is very special."

"From the sound of it, the herbs in your village can make anything smell sweet." Jane was following a new line of questioning. Where is she going with this?

Oulette bragged, "They only grow in my village, perfect soil and humidity. They can make the vilest stink smell sweet. I am using a very small amount to make a special scent for Rita."

"Not that she needs it," the Cheese Pie Man interjected. "My sweet always smells sweet."

Rita smiled at him and squeezed his giant dough hand.

190

Ugh. Enough already. I sighed and picked up my fork. I wiped off the sweat on my forehead with my napkin. Let's get back to business.

"Did you get the ribs at Empire Meats, Mom?" I looked right at the Cheese Pie Man. He stopped chewing but couldn't say anything because his mouth was full. Jane kicked me and gave me a pained look. Mom kept eating.

Now that I had his attention, I wasn't about to stop. "Mom, did you know that Dr. Tallbot is an amphibian expert? He was at our Safari sleepover last night."

"Well, Bert, I never knew you had a keen interest in amphibians. You'll have to talk to my daughters. They see giant frogs in their sleep."

He glared at me and swallowed his giant mouthful. "I'm sure they are just imagining it."

I could see the lump move down his neck like a

191

mouse inside a snake.

"If you like, I can take your girls over to my house one day and they can see my collection of exotic amphibians." He shot a glance at Rita. She nodded in agreement.

"Girls, what do you think of that idea?" Mom looked at us and waited for an answer.

I thought it was nuts, but I wasn't going to say anything. Jane clutched a chunk of my leg so hard I was sure it would bruise. There was no way we would be alone again with the Cheese Pie Man.

I flashed a weak smile. He had won this round.

*****

I grabbed the Cheese Pie Man's plate and was halfway to the kitchen. "Jane and I will clear up the dishes, Mom."

"No, you four go ahead and talk frogs. Maybe then I won't have to listen to it," she laughed. Omelette struggled with the dishes he had stacked into a leaning tower of plates and Mom took the rest of the meat into the kitchen. Jane and I slid out the back door and into the yard; I made a dash to the miniature forest. The screen door slammed shut behind me and I heard the heavy thud of Tallbot's feet on the back porch.

"Not so fast, smarty pants." Smalley had come up behind us more quietly. Her fingers pierced my shoulder like five little swords. She wasn't so great with the sarcasm, but, boy, she had a grip on me. Jane was in front of me and I could see the terrified look on her face.

I tore my shoulder out of Smalley's grip and faced her. "Lady, you are crazy on a stick right side up!" That was a new saying I was trying to start. I thought I'd try it out on Smalley since she was, well, crazy. Smalley glared back at me. Tallbot was on the second last step.

I rubbed my shoulder hard; it throbbed with pain. "Our mom's right inside and the window is open. Do you want me to scream?" I tried to sound tough, but it's hard when you're face to face with the world's tallest woman and her gigantic husband. Tallbot stomped onto the last porch step. His foot landed right where Frogzilla was when... I shot a glance at Jane. No time to think of that now.

"Where's the real formula? And no sugar water this time." His eyes bored a hole through my head as he clomped forward like Godzilla in one of those old-school movies. He looked bigger than last night and couldn't move fast. "It's got to be in this house. Take me to your hiding place. Pretend you're showing me an old science project or something, but take me there." Tallbot was a few clomps away from me.

"We dumped it down the sink," I squealed. With every clomp Tallbot got closer.

"A likely story," Smalley jeered, "since you think you are sleuths or something." She reached for my shoulder again and I ran a few steps back to where Jane was. We stood together, the invincible twin force. Or so I hoped.

"We can do the experiments without it. We just don't need any evidence around ...get it?" She said.

"If it's not harmful to humans then who cares who has the formula? Why not publish a paper about it and make the formula available for the good of the world?" demanded Jane. "Let's make it a dessert 'science topic' why don't we?"

That's enough spunky girl detective routine, I telepathically communicated to my twin. The Cheese Pie Man growled and made two quick stomps closer. His hands reached out as far as they would go. In the background, I could hear Mom talking to Omelette. The sound stopped The Cheese Pie Man in his path.

"One more stunt like that and your mom will be involved—and I don't mean that we'll cut her in on the profits," he whisper-shouted. Spit shot out of the sides of his mouth.

Mom was explaining to Omelette, "Yes, it's my own hot fudge sauce. Calls for a good dollop of vanilla."

Not the vanilla, anything but the vanilla! I pushed past Smalley, hip-checked Tallbot, and dashed up the stairs.

"Mom," I stopped dead, panting in the kitchen. "There's still some in the freezer from last time."

"I'll just whip up a new batch. It'll be hot and fresh. I should probably throw that old batch out anyway." She had the vial, I mean bottle, of vanilla in her hand and was about to open it.

I protested, "Waste not, want not. Ah, remember back in the day, you had to make everything from scratch, couldn't just run to the store? Save for a rainy day." I thought of all the things Mom always said to us when we wanted to throw something out. "You've worked so hard making this dinner, let Jane and me do dessert." I grabbed the vanilla, trying to look like it was no big deal, and slipped it into the pocket of my shorts. *Need to get this out of the house.* Who knew there were so many recipes that called for vanilla?

"Well, isn't that nice? We'll have some coffee outside with Bert and Rita. But the mosquitoes and wasps are so bad this year ..." Mom mused.

Through the kitchen window, I saw the Cheese Pie Man and Smalley in the back yard. He sneered at me. She pinned Jane with her icy glare. A mosquito landed on the Cheese Pie Man's cheek. He slapped his face and left a bloodstain behind. That couldn't make him any happier. They both put their fake smiles on when they saw Mom. We had to solve this mystery fast.

Chapter Sixteen
Super Size Me

Response to Blog Entry: <u>Snakes R Us</u>

Now you're talking! Love the slithering snakes.

Here they'd be sautéed snakes.

They eat everything here.

That would be a good mystery tho – giant snakes,

giant frogs.

Just an idea.

Ciao till later, Dakota.

****

I pedaled hard and gripped the handlebars. It was the next day. A pain shot through my shoulder, a reminder that the Cheese Pie Man and Rita Smalley weren't afraid to hurt people to get what they wanted. What would be their next move?

"What was all that talk about the herb and his village?" I asked Jane.

"I don't know. Making small talk was all." Jane screeched her bike to a halt. "Herbs!"

I crashed into her. "Hey, what's the matter with you!"

She swung her bike around to face me. "That's it. *Sweet-smelling.* That's why Omelette is involved. They need his smelly herbs to counter act the horrible smell of the frog slime for the bug spray. Only he can provide them with it because the herbs grow on his grandma's land."

"That's the last piece of the puzzle,"I exclaimed.

199

We high fived.

But what do we do now? We can't go back to that police officer. He didn't believe us the first time," I said as we rode our bikes around the neighbourhood. Funny how everything looked different now that we knew there were secret plots going on in this town.

"We could try to tell Mom again. I mean, *really* tell her what's going on."

"That would be the third try. That's how we ended up at the Safari sleepover in the first place. Plus, she's bubby-buddy with all three of them. We can't say anything now. Not after the Cheese Pie Man's threat yesterday about Mom, and after what he did to the animal feeder and not to mention..." I remembered I wasn't supposed to mention it, what happened to Jane at the zoo. I continued instead, "We know he's dangerous. If Mom believed us, she'd spill the beans and then she'd be in danger, too– we'd all be in big trouble."

Our voices drifted into the wind. Neither of us wanted to think about the nasty things the Cheese Pie Man would do to our mother. We tried to figure out what to do next as we biked past the mall. Jane didn't even want to stop and go into the pet store. I wondered if her close encounter with the reptile world would turn her off animals for good, or at least for this mystery.

Before we knew it, we were on Main Street. As good a time as any to stop for a Popsicle. We propped our bikes against a lamppost and strolled by Mr. Oulette's restaurant. There was a new sign. *Coming soon ... Frogs' legs from France. Super-sized value. Grand re-Opening!*

"Super Sized Value!" Jane and I said at the same time. We both let out a shout. "That's it."

201

"Giant frog legs!"

"That's what they're doing. Creating giant frogs so Oulette can sell giant frog legs in his restaurant. It wasn't about the bug juice after all," said Jane.

"Dakota was sending us clues. That's what she was getting at. They eat frog legs in France. This is a French restaurant – Giant frog legs!"

I swatted another mosquito. "If Frogzilla were alive he'd eat that..." Then I stopped. Whoops, shouldn't have mentioned Frogzilla. Jane stared at the spot where the mosquito had bitten me. She had a strange look on her face. I could almost see the wheels turning.

"Shortage of frogs, no frogs in the river, tons of mosquitoes, wasps and hornets! I've got it, Cyd."

"Got what, sun stroke? Draw me a map, do the math for me, I don't get it."

"Now, it makes perfect sense. They didn't come

here to create bug juice from frog juice because we have a ton of mosquitoes in our city." Jane sounded like a detective. "It's the opposite. *We have a ton of mosquitoes because they are using local frogs.* We never did figure out where they got all the frogs to do the experiments on. Frogs eat mosquitoes. That's why there are so many insects this summer. *Frogs eat mosquitoes!*" she said again, just to hammer home the point.

"Yeah, remember Dakota's clue about 'what's not getting bit?' the mosquitoes weren't getting bit by the frogs. I told you she gets me."

We jumped on our bikes and pedaled home. We needed to get to Control Central.

****

Jane hovered over the computer. One close call with a snake and finding out local frogs are in danger, and she was more determined than ever. "Hey, let me in on your idea," I begged.

203

"This is more than scrapping off frog slime. They must have used hundreds of frogs in their experiments until they got the formula right. And what do you think they did with the frogs? Got rid of them – like Omelette said, that's what. The latest giant frogs they've created will be eaten. We can't let those, or any more, frogs die. How would Dr. Tallbot like being bio-chemically stretched and then sautéed in barbecue sauce?" She whispered under her breath as she pounded on the keyboard.

Sounded more like what she planned to do with him than a hypothetical.

She tore the page off the printer and handed it to me.

Grand Re-Opening
Chez Oulette

–

Introducing Frogs Legs from France
Super Sized Value –
One leg feeds four
(These were big hoppers!)

–

By Invitation Only

Jane grabbed it back from me and wrote on the bottom, "*Your Honor the Mayor and Mr. Chief of Police, I think you'll find this very interesting. I hope you can find the time to attend. There are frog lives at stake here.*" She signed it: *FoF - A friend of the frogs.*

I screeched, "What are you doing? We're not going to send this to the Mayor and Chief of Police. Are you crazy? What do we do when they show up?" I grabbed the paper back from her and read it again just to make sure it said what I thought it said.

Jane's eyes bulged out of her head. "I've got an idea. We go to the lab and make an antidote to the formula. Then we show up at the grand opening and inject the frogs with the formula. When they start to shrink, the Chief of Police will see what Omelette, and the Cheese Pie Man did, and they'll get arrested."

Holy crazy twin! I rolled my eyes back into my head and hit my forehead with the heel of my hand. "Great plan, Jane. Just one problem. How do we *make* the antidote? We're not exactly scientists. Do I have to remind you that you refused to do experiments on frogs this year? This isn't virtual reality."

"That was different. These frogs need us. They're still alive. We can save them."

She's so far off her rocker she's half way to outer space. "But that still leaves one problem. How do we make the antidote?"

"Easy. We've got the vial of formula, right? We

206

sneak into the lab, find the Cheese Pie Man's notes, and reverse the formula."

"If it was that easy to be a scientist, don't you think everyone would be one?"

"We've got to try something. Think of Frogzilla." Her eyes welled up with tears. She wiped them with the back of her hand. "Think of all the other frogs. If we only save one frog, it would be worth it. Plus, everyone suffers from all the insects that aren't being eaten!"

It was all about Frogzilla! I should have known. Sure, it was also about the evil scientists, the secret experiments on frogs, the possible harm to humankind, and all those pesky mosquitoes, but *mostly* it was about Frogzilla. I wished now more than ever that I hadn't squished him. If I hadn't killed Frogzilla we wouldn't be involved in this mystery. I sighed.

"Besides," I said, "we don't know that harm will come to the people who eat the giant frog legs. People

207

eat frog legs all the time. I hear they taste like chicken."

She wasn't listening. Jane stuffed her favorite Nancy Drew book in her backpack for luck.

I guessed we were going to do this.

I nipped downstairs to the get the formula. The vanilla bottle held our only hope. As lame as it seemed, I agreed to go along with Jane's idea. Half because I felt guilty, and half because I didn't have a better idea. We were almost out of the house when Mom got home. We had to come up with a good excuse to leave before dinner. We had to deliver the invitations to the Chief of Police and the Mayor, and then get to the lab.

"Look girls," she said, "I got an invitation from Mr. Oulette for the grand re-opening of his restaurant. I've never had frog legs before... it's tonight."

We tried to leave while she was still reading. "Where are you off to?"

"We're going to the mall to spend some of our

allowance," I lied. Nancy Drew never had to lie about *her* investigations.

"Make sure you take your key. I'll be at the grand re-opening late. Get some dinner at the mall."

That was easier than I thought it would be. We pedaled like crazy to get to City Hall before the doors shut. A security guard promised he would hand-deliver our invitation to the mayor. At the police station, we left it under the door. I didn't want to have to talk to that police officer again. Besides, the Mayor usually traveled with a police officer.

The sun was setting as we got to the lab. The security guard was not in sight, so we got to Mom's floor pretty easily. Jane raced toward the lab with the bottle of vanilla in her hand. I looked over my shoulder. I was getting good at sneaking around.

Stacks of paper, test tubes, pop cans, and candy wrappers littered the Cheese Pie Man's lab table. Jane shuffled through his papers as if she expected one page to conveniently say, *Giant Amphibian Experiment.*

"He's probably hidden it." I pulled open a drawer and spotted a black notebook. I cracked it open. It was like reading someone's diary. No time to feel guilty, though, especially when the Cheese Pie Man was involved. I flipped through it page by page. It was full of scientific scribbling that looked like another language. Dollar signs across the top of one page looked like a criminal's letterhead. The notes on that page said stuff like: *Frogs, France, M. Oulette, Hormone Experiment,* and more dollar signs.

"Hey look," I squealed. "This must be it." There was a diagram of a frog. I flipped to the next page. Scientific scribbling covered it. The equations took up half a page and there were abbreviated names of chemicals that looked like the lettering we saw in those old English novels in the library. "We can't make an antidote. I don't understand any of this," I tossed the notebook on the lab table.

"But we've got to try. We've got to save the frogs."

"Save the frogs. Ha!" The voice mocked us. "You won't even be able to save yourselves."

We turned around; the Cheese Pie Man blocked the doorway.

***

He clapped his hands loud and hard three times. "Brava. Quite the performance, but the final curtain comes down now." He let out a long hearty laugh.

The Cheese Pie Man had grown. His face swelled up like a cream puff. His pants and shirt stretched to the breaking point. He was so large that he had trouble walking, but he came toward us. That's when we saw Rita Smalley behind him. She was as skinny as ever, and she looked like a snake. I half expected her tongue

211

to dart in and out.

Jane hid behind me. She had the vanilla bottle in one hand, and she squeezed my arm with the other. My legs turned to jelly. It felt like her weight would pull me down. Where was Nancy Drew when you needed her?

"So you think you can save the frogs, do you? Well, well, well." Tallbot tried to saunter toward us but it was more like tree roots moving a stump. "In a couple of hours, the whole town will be sampling Mr. Oulette's exquisite sautéed frog legs and we'll be millionaires. Giant frog legs! Every French restaurant in the country will want them. In the world!" He let out a classic maniacal laugh.

"And it won't be like in France when the hormone started working on people," Tallbot bragged on. "They never would have grown flippers, like it said in the paper. It doesn't have any effect on people.

212

Why look at me. I jabbed myself with the formula and nothing." He stretched out his puffy arms.

Was he kidding us with this?

"No, this time the formula is just right. We'll make a fortune. They said it couldn't be done. I'll show them. No more stinky labs and Bunsen burners for me. They can keep their stinking Supreme Scientist of the Science Department job. I won't need it anymore. I quiver when I think of the export market."

I didn't want to think of him quivering! My thoughts raced to all corners of my brain. I tried to come up with an escape plan. I needed to buy some time while I thought. I'd pepper him with questions since he looked ready to grill. Maybe I could out dumb him – ask a lot of dumb questions until he got annoyed and let us go.

"Why all the stuff with Oulette about the herb that only grows on his grandma's land?"

213

"I love my sweet-smelling Rita, and there are other herbs Oulette rubs into steaks. It will make the frog legs exquisite. He's going to cultivate them and sell bottles of herbs in the restaurant. A nice little side line, if you like."

I didn't. "How did you get them so large? Usually, a growth hormone isn't so dramatic." I don't know how I knew that – it was either my science dweeb gene or ingrained from endless overheard conversations of my parents. Nature or nurture, either way.

"You are right, of course. I would expect no less from the daughter of such esteemed scientists. No, it's a secret ingredient that makes the formula very trade-marketable. I don't mind telling you. It's cayenne."

"Red-hot pepper?" I asked.

Smalley urged, "Bert, forget about these silly girls. Even if they blab, no one will believe them. No one in this town knows what happened in France. Let's keep it that way."

"You can't get away with this," Jane squeaked from behind me. Even in terror, she was spunky. "Everyone will know. Haven't you heard of the Internet? Not to mention the fax machine, the telephone, the telegraph, two soup cans held together by string, smoke signals!"

Whew.

Tallbot made a move to grab us. I shoved the stool in his way.

"So you want to make an antidote and save the frogs." He laughed with the whole force of his body. The floor shook.

"I'll even help you. I'll tell you the antidote. All you would need to do is heat up the formula in that bottle and it would reverse the chemical reaction." He walked closer. His giant hands reached for us. They were so big; he could grab one of us in each hand.

215

"We'll give you back the formula," I shouted.

"Oh no, I wouldn't think of it. I'll tell you what. You keep the bottle. You won't need it where you're going." His laughter bounced off the walls.

"It's too late. You both should have kept your animal-loving noses out of this," Smalley sneered.

The Cheese Pie Man grabbed both of us and headed out of the lab. I struggled and kicked my legs, but they bounced off his stomach. He headed toward the plant vault, followed by Rita Smalley.

"Our Mom will be looking for us," I screamed. You'll never get away with it."

"Don't worry your little detective heads about that." Smalley looked me right in the eye. "I phoned your mom earlier. She's a little too chatty for my taste. Told us about going to the grand re-opening tonight, and you two going to the mall. I pretended I was calling from the mall. Told her we'd just run into you and invited you both to come over for an early dinner to see our collection of amphibians. Then we'd drop you girls home on our way to the opening. She thought it was a peachy idea. By the time she finds you, we'll be halfway to long gone." Her laugh echoed his.

Jane whimpered. I struggled but the air squeezed out of my chest. Still in Tallbot's tight grip, we torpedoed to the plant vault. "You'll be fine in here for a while."

Smalley opened the door, and I screamed. When the Cheese Pie Man threw us in, I searched frantically for something to jam in the door to keep it open. But there was no time. When he shut it, I screamed louder. The padlock clicked into place. He turned off the light switch on the wall outside the vault. The flourescent lights hissed. The plant vault went dark.

217

Chapter Seventeen
The Last Breath

Jane screamed when the last light shimmered and faded.

"Not the *lights*," she pounded her fists on the door of the vault. "It'll be worse without the lights." She screamed for help.

I grabbed her and swung her around to face me. "Calm down. What are you talking about?"

"Don't you get it?" She pulled herself away from me and slumped to the floor. "Plants make oxygen when the lights are on. With the lights off, they don't produce as much oxygen. Before too long there will be no oxygen left. We'll be as limp as that frog in science class."

Jane buried her hands in her face and cried. No snappy comeback from me. I sat down beside her and put my arm around her. She gulped for air between sobs. There was another noise. It was the ventilation system turning off. Already the room felt hotter.

"We'll just have to alternate breaths," I said. "You take one breath and then I'll take the next. We're twins. That should work."

Of course it didn't work. The only light came from the hallway through a small window on the door. It was too high for me to see out of so I knocked some plants off a crate and stood on it. I probably ruined someone's experiment but I didn't care. The glass was as thick as a brick. I knew because I tried to break it.

I didn't know how much time passed but it seemed like Jane sat in the corner crying for hours. I yelled the whole time and my throat was raw. I hoped someone might walk by and hear me. But it was Friday night and no one was in the building. It was stuffy. Could there be much air left? Sweat soaked the back of my tee shirt. There was no way out. I collapsed beside Jane.

I don't know how long I was asleep or if I'd passed out. I brushed my sweat-soaked hair from my forehead and looked up. The air was steamy from our breath. Jane was asleep or worse, I didn't want to think about it. What could we do? It was hopeless. What would Nancy Drew do? She wouldn't give up, especially if she and her twin were running out of time.

I sat up and held my head in my hands. My brain was all fuzzy. I couldn't think straight. Nancy would check every part of the plant vault for a way out

220

or a tool or something. We needed a … I wiped my forehead with my tee shirt then wrung it out. I craved sleep. I was fading fast. So thirsty. Maybe I'd feel better after a nap. I lay down. No, I fought sleep and sat up again. I was afraid I wouldn't wake up.

We needed a … hidden door. A hidden door? What did that mean? I'd been reading way too many mysteries. Wait a minute, that's it. Nancy Drew would look for a hidden door or a trap door. There had to be a way out of here. I rubbed my eyes hard and took a deep breath from the last of the air. One burst of energy was all I needed. It was hot. I didn't know how long we'd been in there. Jane lay beside me. It seemed like she wasn't breathing. My heart stopped beating. "Jane," I shook her hard and waited for her to breathe.

Slowly, she opened her eyes and looked at me. We had to get out of here. I pushed myself off the floor and grabbed on to the plant shelves to pull myself up.

Pots of plants crashed to the ground and splattered over the floor. Finally, I was standing. I held on to the shelves and groped my way to the back of the plant vault like a kid learning to walk. There was a shelf in front of the wall. I grabbed it at the top and toppled it over. Trays of plants fell to the floor. I didn't care. I needed to get Jane out of here.

A thick vine with tons of branches and leaves clung to the wall. I tugged at it and it held fast. It was like a chain link fence. I didn't have much strength left. Sweat streamed down my forehead and stung my eyes. I took a deep breath, caught a hold of a branch, and yanked. The whole thing tumbled down. Behind it, there was a handle. I cleared away the rest of the vines. It was a hidden door, all right! I turned to check on Jane. She had fallen back to sleep. "It won't be long now," I wheezed. "Hold on."

I pushed down on the handle. Nothing

happened. I put both hands on the handle and rammed my whole body weight down on it. The handle inched down. I kept the pressure on so I didn't lose the momentum. The handle stopped and I leaned with all my weight on the door. It flung open and I body-slammed the floor on the other side. The fresh cool air hit me like an ocean wave. I gasped for breath.

It was air-conditioned-laboratory smelling air. The light was dim. We must still be inside. I pulled myself up and used my T-shirt to wipe the sweat from my face. I propped open the door with a broken plant pot, and went back to get Jane. I dragged her over the toppled shelves and vines and into the next room. I laid her down and placed her head on my knee. "Come on Jane, breathe. We're out. It'll be all right."

We weren't trapped in the plant vault anymore, but I didn't know where we were. Jane smiled up at me and breathed deeply. I went for my backpack and put it under Jane's head. Time to find the lights.

I fumbled over the wall close to the door and found a lightswitch. The fluorescent lights hissed, flickered, and then glared into action when I hit the switch. We were in a lab with all the regular stuff. Bunsen burners, test tubes, overhead lamps, and those eye-drop things were on two long tables. It was like a giant lab station. But there was something different about it. I walked cautiously beside the tables. The tables, chairs, clock, and equipment were all old-school. It was like a science museum. I jumped when I felt a hand on my arm.

"Where are we? How did we get out of the plant vault? Oh, my head hurts." Jane pressed her palm against her forehead and leaned into me.

I half-held her up. She was still a bit shaky. "It's a lab attached to the plant vault. But it looks ancient, like an antique store." I caught a glimpse of a picture

224

pinned on the wall behind the lab table. I grabbed it. "Look, it's Seymour, Bert and Rita's dog. You were right. They do have a secret lair and we found it."

"So this is where they were doing the experiments. Not at their lab stations."

"Yeah, all they did there was eat." I remembered the pop cans and candy wrappers. "The Cheese Pie Man must have left his notebook at the other lab as a decoy, to throw us off the scent. Look here," I took a closer look at the lab table. "Different stages of the experiment." I picked up a couple of test tubes and read the labels, "big frogs, super-sized frogs, crazy big frogs, and colossal frogs. Wait a minute; we've been in that hot vault for a while. What if the chemical makeup of the formula is reversed?"

Jane took a quick look at the old-fashioned clock on the wall. "It's eight o'clock now. We were in there for three hours." She strode up the length of the lab

225

table looking for something. "It's worth a try," she said as she grabbed a package of syringes and stuffed them into her backpack. "The grand re-opening will just be getting started. Let's go."

The door of the lab led to the hallway. I turned back to look at it. The sign on the door read *Maintenance*. No wonder no one suspected anything. The sunlight hurt my eyes when we got outside; the summer sun was still high in the sky. We hopped on our bikes. I squished my bike helmet over my sweaty hair.

Next stop, Chez Oulette!

Chapter Eighteen
The Last Straw

From the street, we heard party sounds. We looked through the window. A man in a beret played an accordion, and people ate French appetizers. Well, *hors d'oeuvres* in French. It didn't look like giant frog legs they were snacking on, but it sure smelled good. I hadn't eaten since lunch. Everyone laughed and smiled. Little did they know about the evil plot cooked up by Omelette and the Cheese Pie Man. They were unwittingly about to eat growth-hormone and cayenne-pepper-altered entrées.

Sure, once a year we'd feast on genetically manipulated cherries that Mom's scientist friend from Vancouver sent. And grocery stores had foods that were bio-chemically changed, but people knew what they were buying. They had ethics committees. Mom and Dad always yawned on about that at the dinner table. Not to mention rules and approvals. Maybe what the Cheese Pie Man did wasn't illegal. But who said he could use all the local frogs, and what was with all the sneaking around? That's what got me. That and well, he was just plain mean.

"Can you see the Chief of Police and the Mayor?" asked Jane.

I looked around for them. I had only ever seen them on television. I pointed, "Right there. The Chief of Police is talking to Omelette and the Mayor is talking to Mom."

We turned to look at each other. How was Mom

going to react to all of this?

There was no turning back now. We could hear everything through the front door that was propped open.

"Ladies and gentlemen." It was Omelette. He motioned for the man in the beret to stop playing the accordion. "I would like to welcome you to the grand re-opening of Chez Oulette. I am happy to be a part of your community. Tonight the pièce de résistance is our giant frog legs from France. For the past two hundred years in a small mountain village in France, peasants lovingly raised these frogs for their flavour and size. Now thanks to me you have the opportunity to taste one of France's greatest treasures. For your dining pleasure, they have been imported. I have prepared them with herbs that only grow in my village."

He winked at the Cheese Pie Man.

"But first I would like to show you the magnificent

229

frogs that the legs came from."

"What is he doing?" Jane nudged me and peered closer in the window.

The Cheese Pie Man was there in all his cheese pie glory. He pushed a big cart filled with frogs, like in a restaurant that serves lobsters, only bigger. The frogs were about half the size of the ones in the greenhouse, but they were still big. The frogs flopped around in the cart that was filled with a little bit of water.

"This is it. It's now or never."

Before I could stop her, Jane burst through the front door of the restaurant. I was right behind her.

"Stop! Don't let him kill those frogs. They don't deserve to die."

Everybody stopped what they were doing and looked at Jane. Some people smirked, and others laughed. I must admit, if she weren't my twin, I would've laughed as well. She looked like a pint-sized activist. She held the vanilla bottle in her hand, over her head, like a stick of dynamite. Her sweat soaked hair pressed against her forehead, and her tee shirt was covered with plant and dirt grime. Usually, I could read her mind, but I had no idea what she would do next.

"Jane, what is the meaning of this?" Our mother's voice cut through the air slowly like a bread knife through a stale bagel. Now we were in for it. "What are you two doing here?"

"They're not who you think they are, Mom. We went to the police, but they wouldn't listen." Jane turned to plead with the crowd of people who stopped in mid-bite. "In the lab ... he's been creating giant amphibians. He tried to kill us. Twice! We thought it was about the herbs and frog juice for bug juice, but it's not. Just look at how many mosquitoes there are! They lied to you."

"What are you talking about? Who? This time

231

you girls have gone too far." Mom strode toward us. "I thought Bert and Rita were going to drop you home." There was a hint of doubt in Mom's voice, but she was still mad.

"Him," Jane pointed at Dr. Tallbot. "The Cheese Pie Man. He locked us in the plant vault."

All eyes turned to Tallbot. His face was so red with anger I thought it would implode. I guess he didn't expect to see us so soon. Then, his face turned as sweet as a sunrise.

"There is no Cheese Pie. This must be some kind of child's game ... the imagination gone wild, you know, with television and computer games."

He turned to the crowd. "Mr. Oulette is a successful business man, and I am a well-known scientist. I think maybe their mother, who is also a scientist, has told them stories." His smile disappeared and he glowered at Mom.

232

That's when I got mad. "Don't try to blame this on my mother. I saw them, too. Giant frogs. You and your buddies tried this experiment in France. Dr. Smalley's in on it too. They broke the regulations and people got sick. They did the experiments in secret. They didn't go to any ethics committee. And, they went through a lot of frogs in this town. That's why there's a bumper crop of insects this summer. They have a secret lair – I mean, lab."

Jane piped back up. "They lied to our Mom, and they ate ribs at our house, and the snake ..." She put her hands around her neck to mime strangulation.

Okay, now she was losing it. My turn to step in again.

"We have the antidote right here. We'll show you." I grabbed Jane's backpack and pulled out the package of syringes. I tore it open and handed Jane a syringe. She fumbled the top off the vanilla bottle. The

233

top landed on the floor and bounced a couple of times. That was the only sound in the room. All eyes were on Jane. Sweat dripped down her forehead. She struggled with the syringe, stuck it in the top of the bottle, and slowly pulled the plunger up. Her hands shook.

"We'll inject the frogs and see if they shrink. Then we'll know the truth." She held the syringe high in the air. The Mayor checked her Blackberry, and the Chief of Police swatted a mosquito on his arm. Some people went back to eating. Oulette tried to get the music started again. But he was interrupted by what happened next. Jane was ready. She held the syringe up.

"No!" The shout was like a cannon ball blast out of the Cheese Pie Man's mouth. He lunged across the room and grabbed for the syringe. At the same time, Jane ran toward the frogs. They collided and the syringe went straight into the Cheese Pie Man's hand.

He recoiled in pain.

"What's going on here?" the Chief of Police shouted, "I've had enough of this…"

Finally, I thought. Now we'll get some action.

"… you girls should be ashamed of yourselves. Accusing these three of such a crime. Besides, I'm hungry. I've been thinking about those frog legs all week. We'll have your mother take you home now." The Chief motioned for Mom. She headed toward us looking angrier than when I accidentally washed her angora sweater.

"Come, girls. This little charade is over," she herded us to the door like sheep.

People milled around, confused. They looked like they wanted to get back to the party. The accordion man squeezed the air out of his instrument, warming it up for another tune.

Then something strange happened. A silence fell

235

over the restaurant. It was eerie. Time slowed down to the pace of a dripping tap. I heard a soft croak. Then a hissing noise, like the air let out of a tire tube. Everyone stared at the Cheese Pie Man. His face twisted up in pain. He had pulled the needle out of his hand, but not before the antidote shot into his body. He shrank. Slowly, like a balloon with a leak or a bike tire when you ran over glass, he crumpled onto the floor with a groan.

He flopped on his back and let out a noise...

Chapter Nineteen
Freedom From Fryers

"Ribbit."

"I knew it," I said to Jane. "The formula *does* work on humans."

No one moved. The Cheese Pie Man would soon be back to his normal size and we would have to call him the Thin Crust Man.

The Chief of Police spoke. "I'm going to have to take you in for questioning, Dr. Tallbot. Dr. Smalley and Mr. Oulette, you'd better come too. There's something funny going on around here and I aim to find out what it is." He swatted a mosquito on his neck, and then looked at his hand. He shook his head. "The frogs, too. They'll be coming with me." He surveyed the giant frogs, "I better call for some back up."

I'd like to see *those* in the back of a police car.

"What is going to happen to the frogs?" Jane cried.

I struck the heel of my hand against my forehead. Jane just wouldn't give up.

He turned to us. "If you have any more of that antidote I'll take that as well. Maybe the folks in the lab can mix up some more and we can save these frogs. If we can get them back down to their normal size we'll set them free at the swamp."

I looked down at my feet. My lucky red shoes looked back up at me. Was it the shoes, Nancy Drew or two twin brains being better than one? I didn't know.

I was just happy it was over. Our first mystery solved. Nancy Drew would be proud, but it might take Mom a little longer.

Jane sighed a sigh of relief and smiled, deep inside. I could feel it. It was a smile that meant all was right with the world, well at least the frog world, and at least for tonight. What was next for the Cyd and Jane Files?

Turned out the Chief of Police was right. The frog antidote worked on some of the frogs and the formula started wearing off on the rest.

The town made Jane and me heroines. There was an article in the newspaper, Local Girls Save Frogs From the Fryer. They gave us a special citation presented by none other than Deputy Dan and his police dog Dawber.

I never told anyone about getting the idea to escape the plant vault from all the Nancy Drew books

239

we'd read. She had some good advice, for a fictional character.

We blogged about the whole adventure. We even posted pictures of the Cheese Pie Man *before* and *after* along with two pictures of frogs *before* and *after*. Dakota said next time let her in on the mystery.

Our next blog entry headline will be: *Maybe Science Really was Cool like our Parents Have Been Telling us for Ages, Especially When You Can Use It to Solve a Mystery.*

The police took the frogs down to the river to have a good feast on mosquitoes. That was a relief to the whole, itchy town. Then they put Jane in charge of finding new homes for the leftover frogs. She made up a couple of rules. No evil scientists need apply, and you must never have killed a frog with your bare feet. Well, that let me out of adopting one. I noticed that Jane had put aside a special frog for herself and named it Frogzilla, the Sequel.

Bert Tallbot, Rita Smalley and Mr. Oulette were arrested and charged with using their brains for evil purposes rather than good and crimes against amphibians – or something like that. I think the cops even threw in a charge of being crazy on a stick right side up. Mom promised to believe us next time we came up with a mystery. With our first mystery solved, I was itching, and this time not from a mosquito bite. I itched to come up with another adventure!

But maybe we'd take a break first, and enjoy Jane's new frog. Besides, we were off to join Dad in London for the rest of the summer.

If there is one thing I learned from all this, it's: *Look before You Leap on top of a Live Frog and Squish Its Guts out with Your Foot.* It's a little long for a blog entry title, but I think you get my meaning.

Dead Frog Discussions

on evil

When a writer creates an evil character, the character's qualities can't be all bad or it would be a "one-sided" or "stock" character. Even if they are evil, characters need to be well-rounded and three-dimensional.

What are some of the good qualities of Dr. Tallbot, aka the Cheese Pie Man?

Do these qualities make him a well-rounded (no pun intended) character?

Why is the character of Rita Smalley not as well developed?

What's a pun?

on theme

What is the theme of the book?

How does the interconnectedness of humans and the environment relate to the theme?

Can you give examples of this theme in the book?

on balance

The girls' cat is called Yin. In Chinese philosophy, the concept of Yin and Yang is used to describe things that are opposing forces in nature (for example winter is yin to summer's yang) and opposites within a whole (like a hot fudge sundae – both hot and cold).

How does the concept of Yin and Yang apply to the characters in the book? Which characters does it apply to?

on conflict

Characters need both inner and outer conflict. Outer conflicts are the things that happen to the character that s/he has no control over. Outer conflicts move the story along (for example, rainstorm, car crash, curfew). Inner conflict is what drives the character (for example love, revenge, justice).

What is Cyd's inner conflict?

How does it drive her actions in the story?

on genetic engineering

Genetic engineering is when a scientist manipulates or changes the genes and creates something else like synthetic insulin, vaccines and crops that can resist pests. Scientists create something through biochemistry by changing the structure and function of the cell.

What is a cell?

What is DNA?

How are the two connected?

It's not against the law for scientist to use genetic engineering or biochemistry to create things that they believe will benefit society. But, some people think it's wrong and they have ethical issues with it.

What is the difference between a legal issue and an ethical issue?

Why aren't ethical issues right or wrong?

on characters

Frogzilla the pet frog dies in the opening sentences of the story and Nancy Drew, who is already a fictional character, is not really in the book, but the twins talk about her. In a way, Frogzilla and Nancy Drew are characters.

What is the role of Frogzilla in the book?

What is the role of Nancy Drew in the book?

How do they affect the actions of the characters?

on fear

Cyd and Jane, and maybe their mother, are in danger in the book. There are times when Cyd and Jane feared for their safety and the safety of the frogs.

What role did fear play for Cyd and Jane?

Did other characters feel fear?

How did fear motivate the characters?

on beliefs

It would be easy for Cyd and Jane to ignore what the scientists are doing and just relax for the summer, ride around on their bikes, go to the pool and eat ribs (or maybe dig into the frogs' legs). But they think what the scientists are doing is wrong.

They believe finding out what the scientist are up to and saving the frogs is the right thing to do. The right thing to do is not always the easy thing to do. Do you agree with this?

Think of examples from your own life where making the right choice was difficult.

In some countries and cultures, people eat frogs' legs. What may be strange to you may be breakfast to someone in another culture.

How do things like our culture, our beliefs, our environment (for example, the weather can determine which crops can grow), and our attitudes determine what we eat and how we eat it?

What is the strangest food you have eaten?

Why did you think it was strange?

In the book Cyd and Jane don't follow a certain religion, but they have learnt about many of the religions of the world. What is the difference between being spiritual and being religious?

How many different religions can you name?

Have you participated in different religious or spiritual ceremonies or celebrations?

How does our religion or spiritual views shape the way we see the world?

on haikus

Cyd and her friend Dakota write Haikus to each other over the twin's blog.

Why are the Haikus important to the story?

In other words, what purpose do the Haikus serve?

What is a Haiku?

Have you ever written one?

Try writing one now.

about the author
Jan Markley

photo © 2009 Ashley Bristowe

Jan Markley is a writer living in Calgary, Alberta, Canada. *Dead Frog on the Porch* is her début novel for young readers. Growing up she was a voracious reader of Nancy Drew mysteries and enjoyed visiting the library, where she would stretch her library card to the limit.

Jan previously worked as a print and broadcast journalist. She writes creative non-fiction and has had personal essays published in the *Globe and Mail* and *West World*. She has a Master of Arts degree in Cultural Anthropology, and enjoys traveling and discovering other cultures.

248

Check out Jan's website at:
www.deadfrogontheporch.com

acknowledgements

This story started as a "write an incident from your childhood" exercise, and grew chapter by chapter into a novel. Members of my writers' group and Peter Carver's Writing for Children workshop in Toronto saw the first version. Thanks to members of the Kensington Writers' Group in Calgary who gave me valuable feedback on later versions of the manuscript. You writers rock, as always.

Thanks to my young readers Teaghan, Diane, and Lydia for their feedback and advice to use exciting words. To my friend Amber, who is an editor/writer trapped in the body of a voracious reader, thanks for your feedback.

Thanks to my sisters, Nancy and Maureen, my brothers (and brothers-in-law), aunts and numerous cousins for their ongoing support and encouragement of my writing over the years. I acknowledge all my nieces and nephews, for their youthful, yet wise advice. To my friends, colleagues, and members of the writing community, your interest and support over the years was valued and appreciated. And always, thanks to my childhood friends Sandra, Margaret, Ruth, and Nancy M2 for their support in everything I undertake in life.

Thanks to Crystal and Jared for loving dead frogs, believing in the project, and launching the Megabyte Mystery series.

Thanks Nancy Drew. Fictional character that you are, you were real to many of us young readers who admired your independence and bravery.

To my childhood friend Jane, sorry I killed your frog. It was an accident, really!

249

Coming Fall 2010 from Gumboot Books

The next megabyte mystery by Jan Markley

Dead Bird through the Cat Door

Dead birds? Stolen cats? C'est what? When Cyd and Jane's cat Yin gets kidnapped – that's when it gets personal.

Once again, Cyd and her animal-loving twin Jane are up to their bird beaks in intrigue, cracking the latest Megabyte Mystery. The director of the bird sanctuary, Aviary Finch, is stealing cats to kill birds. But why? Their new sidekick Todd–whose side is he on anyway?

The twins use the latest technology to crack this case but it's Shakespeare's Macbeth *who helps solve the crime. Methinks the culprits doth protest too much! Will Cyd and Jane save the sanctuary, free the birds, and return the cats to their natural habitat of their owners' laps? It's predator-eats-predator when evil meets crazy!*

visit www.gumbootbooks.com for updates

about gumboot books

Gumboot Books is a socially and environmentally responsible company. We measure our success by the impact we have on the lives and dreams of our authors and illustrators, the impact we have on the environment, and the ways in which we help to enrich the lives of everyone who reads our books.

If you would like to see how we are reducing our ecological footprint, and how we are supporting community numeracy and literacy projects, please visit us online at www.gumbootbooks.com

ordering information

Please visit us online at

www.gumbootbooks.com

for information on how to order our books.

251

LaVergne, TN USA
15 March 2011
220253LV00001B/10/P